VERONICA & SUSAN

VERONICA & SUSAN

Telepathic Connection of Two Friends

A tale of two friends

VICTORIA A. GIBSON

Veronica & Susan

Copyright © 2023 by Victoria A. Gibson. All rights reserved.

No part of this publication may be reproduced, stored in a retrieval system or transmitted in any way by any means, electronic, mechanical, photocopy, recording or otherwise without the prior permission of the author except as provided by USA copyright law.

The opinions expressed by the author are not necessarily those of URLink Print and Media.

1603 Capitol Ave., Suite 310 Cheyenne, Wyoming USA 82001
1-888-980-6523 | admin@urlinkpublishing.com

URLink Print and Media is committed to excellence in the publishing industry.

Book design copyright © 2023 by URLink Print and Media. All rights reserved.

Published in the United States of America

Library of Congress Control Number: 2023919886
ISBN 978-1-68486-562-8 (Paperback)
ISBN 978-1-68486-563-5 (Digital)

23.09.22

I LIKE TO DEDICATE THIS BOOK TO MY FAMILY. TO MY CHILDREN WHO WERE THERE WHEN NO ONE ELSE WAS. TO MY PARENTS, WHO LET ME KNOW I COULD DO ANYTHING, I SET MY MIND TO AND TO MY WONDERFUL HUSBAND, TERRENCE.

ALL MY WONDERFUL GRANDCHILDREN. WHOM I WROTE STORIES FOR WHEN THEY WERE YOUNG. BEST OF ALL TO MY BEST FRIEND IN ALL THE WORLD VERONICA

CHAPTER ONE

I woke up this morning covered with blood. I couldn't figure out how it had gotten there. I thought that maybe my period had started during the night, but it couldn't be that it was too early for that to happen. So, I went into the bathroom to take a shower. The water felt good on my body. I stood there, letting the warm water run down my body, trying to figure out where the blood came from and how it got there. I couldn't figure it out. Finally, I got out of the shower and went into the bedroom to dry my hair and think. But I couldn't stay in there it was too much blood. So, I got dressed and went to the kitchen for a cup of coffee. I didn't know what I was going to do. I wish I had someone to talk to, but there was no one. I was an only child, and my parents had died last year in a car crash. I thought about my best friend Susan, who I hadn't seen in years, wondering what she would say about this. I thought about what my mother would tell me to do. So, I got dressed and did it. I walked to the twelfth street police station for some help.

"I would like to talk to someone about an accident," I told the officer at the desk.

"What kind of accident?" he asked.

"I don't know. That's why I need to talk to someone."

"Where did the accident take place?" he wanted to know.

"I don't know."

"When did the accident happen?"

"I don't know. Last night I think."

"Why do you think that there was an accident?"

"That's what I want to explain to someone. When I woke up, this morning I was cover in blood and I couldn't figure out how it got there. I thought it was my period, but it wasn't. I couldn't figure out how it got there. My mother told me if there was a serious problem or an accident that I should go to the police, that's why I'm here. I need to talk to someone."

"Wait here; I'll find someone to help you." The officer said.

As he left, I sat there wondering what I would say that wouldn't make me sound crazy.

"Jones, I got a young lady out there who says she woke up this morning covered in blood and she doesn't know how it got there."

"Oh yeah, so what do you want me to do about it?"

"Go out and talk to her; see if there is anything to what she says."

"What her name I didn't ask, and she didn't offer. Just go out and talk to her."

I sat there and waited; it seemed like it was taking forever. Finally, the officer came back with a female officer. I stood to wait for them to get close to me.

"Miss, sorry, but I didn't get your name."

"Smith, Veronica Smith."

"Miss Smith, I'm Officer Jones. What can I do for you?"

"It's like I told the other officer I woke up this morning, and there was blood everywhere, and I don't know how it got there. So I try to remember everything I did last night; every minute is accounted for."

"So, where do you think the blood comes from Ms.Smith?"

"I don't know. If you come over to my apartment, you will see what I'm talking about."

"Where do you live, Miss Smith?"

"Veronica, please call me Veronica."

"Where do you live, Veronica?"

"I live three blocks from here. I didn't know what to do so I came here to talk to someone. I didn't clean it up so you could see it and tell me what I needed to do."

"I'll tell you what, you go home, and we will get the crime lab over to take some pictures and blood sample. We should be over there in about an hour."

"Can I wait and go back with you? I don't want to go back by myself."

"If you want, it's going to be about an hour, like I said."

"That's okay. I'll wait. I'll sit right over there out the way and wait for you."

I sat there; it seemed like forever, but it was only about forty-five minutes, so that wasn't long. Officer Jones came back. "Veronica, sorry it took so long, but I told you it would be about an hour."

"That's okay. Can we go now?

"Sure," she said. Let's go.

I took her back to my apartment. When we got there, I was surprised to see it was clean. The bed was made, and the dishes were a wash, and I couldn't remember doing any of it.

"So, where's all this blood you told us was here?"

"I don't know. When I left, it was all over the place."

"Who could have cleaned it up?" she asked

"I don't know," I said, puzzled.

"Are you sure this is where you were last night in this apartment?" she asked.

"Yes, this is my apartment. I don't understand what happened to all the blood?"

"Veronica, do you know that filing a false police report is a crime?"

"I didn't report a false crime. There was blood all over the place. In here, in the bedroom, in the bath, and even in the kitchen everywhere. I don't know what happened. I didn't clean it up."

"Then who did?" She asked. Alright, boys, if it was as much blood as she says there is bound to be some left on something, let's get started.

"It took well over an hour, and we checked every spot in that apartment and couldn't find a thing, sergeant. I don't think there was ever anything there."

"What did she say?" The sergeant asked.

She insisted that everything she told us was the truth.

"Where is she now?"

"We left her at the apartment."

"Let's check and see if there was a crime in her neighborhood last night. And let's check her out as well while we're at it," he said.

CHAPTER TWO

I couldn't understand what had happened. Where did all the blood go? I try to figure it out; maybe I just imagine it or dreamt it. I just didn't know. That couldn't be right. I know I didn't dream it; something else was going on. I walk around for a while. I called my job and told them that I wouldn't be in that day for work. I very seldom take a day off, so that was alright. I walked around trying to, figuring out what was going on. I went over everything I did the night before but still couldn't figure out where the blood came from or where it went, for that matter.

It was one o'clock, so I went to a fast food place for some lunch. I sat there, trying to figure out what was going on. Was I going crazy? Maybe I just thought I seem all that blood; I don't know. All I knew was I had to find the answer.

I sat there longer than I thought because two hours had passed when I looked at my watch. I was surprised; usually, they don't let you stay in one of those places that long. As I was leaving, I bumped into a girl I hadn't seemed since high school. I couldn't remember her name; as hard as I tried, I just couldn't remember her. It's funny because we used to hang out together all the time. We stood there talking about how long it had been since we seemed one another.

"So, how long had it been?" I asked her.

"Ages the last time was at Betty's party about six years ago."

"Six years? Are you sure?" I asked her.

"Remember you were telling me you were starting this new job with this big firm downtown. How is that going, by the way? Meet any interesting men yet?" she asked.

"Girl, you know if I had, I would have told you the minute we started talking. You know I can't keep anything for you." Besides, I didn't take that job. I started a small catering and event planning service. What about you?

"Will I did, and Ronnie he is to die for."

(I still couldn't figure out who she was. She looked familiar, but I couldn't place her. She looked so different to me for some reason.)

"Oh yeah? I hope he not like Bobby was back in high school," I said. (Not understanding how I remember all this about her and not her.)

"Bobby? I forgot all about him. You still remember him?"

"I sure do the way you used to call me every night and talk about him. How could I forget?"

"I know, weren't we a couple of airheads back then?"

"You were the airhead, not me; I would just listen to you talk about Bobby this and Bobby that and how Bobby asked you to go here or there with him."

"How is Bobby, by the way?" she asked.

"I don't know; last I heard, he got married to that Girl Lillian that was two grades behind us. I think they got about six kids now, or so I heard."

"Look at the time she said, looking at her watch, I got to go, but it was good running into you like this, please stay in touch. Here's my card, call me in a couple of days and maybe we can go out for a drink or something, okay? I got to go. Call me," she said as she left.

CHAPTER THREE

I stood there looking at her, wondering who she was, and what was her name? I just couldn't remember it. How could I remember so much about her and not remember her name? I looked down at the card she had given me, Susan Brown, personal assistant supervisor to a Wall Street firm president.

Susan! Susan Brown! I remember her now. We used to get into so much trouble when we were growing up. I was at her house, or she was over to mine. How could I not remember her name? We were so closed when we were kids. How could I have forgotten her name? (I watched her walk down the street, not knowing that in a couple of days, she would be found dead in her apartment.)

I turned and started walking in the other direction, still wondering how I could've forgotten Susan's name. I couldn't wait to talk to her again; we had a lot to catch up on. Speaking to Susan had made me forget all about the scene in my apartment that morning. I couldn't wait to talk to her later that night.

It was six o'clock when I got back to my place. I went to check my messages. Susan had called asking me to call her back as soon as I got her message (I never thought about how she got my number because I hadn't given it to her). I was putting my packages away when the phone rang. It was Susan.

"I was just thinking about calling you. I just got your message, so what's up?" I asked her.

"Nothing, it was just so good seeing you today that I felt like talking to you, that's all. Is it okay? I mean, if you are busy or have something to do, we can talk at another time."

"Don't be silly; this is the best time right now. I was going to call you myself later tonight. I can't believe how long it's been since we talked to one another. How many years has it been again?"

"Too many. I just wanted to catch up on all the things that have happened since we last saw each other," Susan said.

"If you had told anyone in high school that we would lose touch with each other, they would drop dead, not believing it," I laughed.

"I know. It's funny how time gets away from you. I thought a lot about you, Ronnie, wondering where you were and what you were doing. It was so good seeing you today. I didn't want to wait any longer to talk to you. You were the only one I could talk to when we were kids. Is that still true? Can I still talk to you, Ronnie?"

"Yes, Suzy, you can talk to me anytime you want."

"Don't call me that. You know how I hate to be called Suzy."

"I know, but you sounded too serious just now, and I wasn't ready for it." (I could almost see Susan frowning.)

"Same old Ronnie, you haven't changed a bit, still likes to start things slow."

"Well, not slow, but it's been a while since I've seen you. I would like to know what you have been doing before we get too serious, okay?"

"Fine by me," she said.

"So, what have you been up to, my blue eyes friend?" I asked her.

"You did use to call me that. I forgot all about that."

"So what is going on? Tell me; I want to hear all about Everything you've been doing since I last saw you," I said to her.

"Remember, our last year of high school? Back then, we thought we would be able to conquer the world," Susan said.

"You didn't do so bad," I told her.

You were talking about Robert Miller today, and it started me wondering about how things turned out for us." Ignoring what I just said to her.

"Robert Miller, when did you start calling Bobby, Robert?" What's going on? You wouldn't even do that in high school.

You said he didn't look like a Robert to you; that's why we called him Bobby. We were the only ones who did. He wouldn't let anyone else call him anything but Robert."

"That right, he wouldn't," Susan said with a smile in her voice.

"Remember that time he was going out for the track team, and we were in the stands calling his name and talking about his legs? Remember when the team started calling him sticks because we did." I said.

"Yeah, he was the best runner they had," she said.

"He came over to the bleachers and asked us very politely not to call him that. His name was Robert, and he liked to be addressed that way. We looked at each other, then at him, and started to laugh. That's when you said, " No, you don't look like a Robert to me, more like a Bobby, and that's what we shall call you, Bobby." So we started calling him Bobby from that day on."

"So why are you calling him Robert now? It sounds funny coming from you."

"You know, I forgot how we came to call him Bobby. Remember how thin he was?"

"He sure was, but he was the fastest runner I'd ever seen. And what about Carol Watson?"

"Carol Watson?" Susan asked, sounding puzzled.

"You remember the girl who thought that every guy who looked at her wanted her. She had long blond hair and green eyes.

She thought we weren't good enough to breathe the same air that she was breathing or walk the same planet she was walking on. Remember when she was running for homecoming queen and said," I know I'm going to win, so no one else needed to run."

"Remember I talked you into running against her for homecoming," I said.

"Can you believe I won?" Susan asked.

"Yes, I always knew you could. Besides, no one liked Carol Watson but the few friends she had. Carol ran for prom queen and lost to you again. She hated you for that. Remember what she said?"

We hadn't heard the last of her," Susan said absent-mindedly. "So what? That was years ago.

"Remember she came to us after graduation and told us she was going to Paris for her graduation present from her parents for two weeks. And you told her we were going to Hawaii for a month. She looked like she was going to explode. It rained the whole two weeks she was in Paris. We had so much fun in Hawaii. You got that beautiful tan, and Carol was jealous of you for that."

"I couldn't believe my parents let me go," I said.

"I know enough about Carol Watson. What have you been up to, Ronnie?" Susan wanted to know.

CHAPTER FOUR

"Well, after you went to New York, I stayed here and opened my own catering business."

"How is that working out?" she wanted to know.

"It's okay, but I had to get a real job to support myself until it got up and running the way I wanted it to."

"Oh, where do you work?" Susan asked.

"I am a loan officer at a bank downtown."

"Do you like it?" Susan asked.

"It pays the bills," I said, looking around my apartment.

"What about you? How's your job going?" I asked.

"My job, what to tell you about my job?" she said, sounding sad.

"Well, the truth, silly," I told her.

"Only if it was that easy. Ronnie, you knew I always wanted to go to New York, and I didn't want to be a man trophy because of my look, but that just what happened. I went out a couple of times with a client, and that when it started."

"That when what started?" I wanted to know.

"I didn't know he was married, Susan said. He brought me the apartment where I live in New York." He brought me everything we ever talked about getting for ourselves. Remember when we were young, and we would sit and talk about the things we wanted and the places we wanted to go?" Well, Ronnie, I went to those places, and he brought me those things. Ronnie, believe me, I didn't know he was married.

"Okay, I believe you, Susan. What's wrong?"

Well, a couple of months or so ago, I ran into him and his wife at Bloomingdale. I didn't know she was his wife; she wasn't standing with him. I saw him and went over and kissed him.

"Darling, what a surprise!" I said. He gave such a look. "Aren't you glad to see me?" I asked

Then this beautiful young lady walked over and asked him who I was.

"This is a young lady from the firm I do business with," he told her.

"Oh, really?" she said. I never heard you mention her before. What's her name?

"It's Susan, Susan Brown, I believe. "I thought I told you about her."

"No, you never mention her before," she said.

And then she told me she was his wife. Oh, Ronnie, I didn't know what to do. I just stood there looking at her. Then I said the most stupid thing.

"Which was?" I asked

"Your wife? You never told me that you were married," I said to him.

"Why should he tell you he's married?" she asked.

"No reason. I'm surprised, that's all," I said. I could tell she knew something was going on between us. I turned and walked away. I know I should have said something else, but I couldn't think of what to say, so I just left.

"It doesn't sound to me like you did too much harm," I told her.

"But I did. I didn't say goodbye, or it was nice meeting you or anything. I just left."

"So, what happened?" I asked her.

A couple of days later, he came by the apartment. I was glad to see him, but he was so angry with me. He wanted to know why I came up to him that day in Bloomingdale.

"I didn't know that she was your wife," I said. I didn't even know you were married.

"You shouldn't walk up on me like that in public. I had to try to explain to Miriam exactly who you were."

"What did you tell her about me?"

"Just what I told her in the store. You were just someone who works at the firm I do business with; then she wanted to know why you called me darling? I had a hard time coming up with an answer to that one. One, she would believe anyway."

"Did you come up with an answer for her?"

"Yes. I believe I did," he said.

"Do you mind telling me what it was?" I asked him.

"I told her we had work late one evening, and we went out for dinner; you had too much to drink, and it was just a little joke of yours."

"And she believed that?" I asked him, looking dumfounded

"Yes, don't let this happen again," he said.

"Well, I guess that wasn't too bad," I said.

"But it was." Susan said. "Oh, Ronnie, you just don't know how bad."

"Then why don't you tell me," I said.

I didn't know what was worst, being called a drunk or her thinking I was an whore.

CHAPTER FIVE

"Things became very tense around the office after that. It was like everyone knew what was going on. I would get these looked from the people I worked with before. Finally, I stopped getting the big clients I was getting. Sometimes weeks would go by before I got any clients at all. So the next time he came over, I asked if he knew what was going on.

"Did you tell my boss about what happened at Bloomingdale?" I asked him.

"I may have said something," he said.

"Is that the reason I haven't been getting any work?" I asked him.

"I wouldn't know. I don't work there. I'm just a client."

"Look, let's forget about it for now. You know I'm married, so let's just go on from here," he said.

"I thought you loved me? I thought that one day we would get married. But I see now that's impossible."

"Married? When did I say anything about getting married?" he asked, turning on me.

"You didn't. I just thought that one day we might," I told him.

"I don't know why you would think that. It never crossed my mind."

Susan started to cry. I didn't know what to say. Susan was my best friend; I hadn't seemed her in years. I didn't know what was going on in her life. I didn't know what to say or if I should say anything at all.

"Ronnie, what should I do? She asked me.

"I don't know," I said. Then, I thought, why don't you come stay with me for a couple of weeks? Do you have vacation time coming up?"

"That's a fanatic idea. Work is slow right now, at least for me anyway. I'll be there in a couple of days if that okay?"

"That fine. We can go to some of our old hang out."

"That sounds great. I'll call you in a couple of days and tell you what flight I'm on."

What flight you're on? Susan, I just saw you today. You're right in town. Susan? Susan!"

I called into the phone, but I got no answer. The line was dead. I wanted to call her back, but I didn't know where she was staying in town. So I decided to call her mother.

Hello, Mrs. Brown, this is Veronica Smith, Susan's friend. Do you remember me?

"Of course, I remember you, Veronica. How are you?"

"Fine," I told her.

"And how are your parents?" Mrs. Brown asked.

"They died in a car accident last year," I said.

"I'm sorry to hear that," she said.

"Mrs. Brown, the reason I'm calling is I talked to Susan a little while ago, and she said that she would come to visit me in a couple of days. But I just saw her earlier today downtown. I was wondering if she was staying with you. If she is, I would like to talk to her, please."

"She's not here. I didn't know she was even in town."

"You didn't? I saw her today, and in fact, we just got off the phone. She said she would be flying out in a couple of days, and I wanted to ask her about that; if she's here, why did she have to fly in?"

"I don't know. I haven't heard from Susan for a couple of weeks now," her mother said.

"That's strange, well maybe she'll call me back. But if you hear from her before I do, could you please have her call me?" I asked her.

"I will. It was good hearing from you again, Veronica," she said.

"Thank you, Mrs. Brown; it was good talking to you again too," I said and hung up.

CHAPTER SIX

A week passed, and I still hadn't heard from Susan. So I called her mother back. "Mrs. Brown, this is Veronica, Susan's friend? I was calling to see if you heard from Susan yet? I'm still waiting for her call."

"Oh, Veronica, I'm sorry I meant to call you. Susan is dead," Mrs. Brown said.

"Did you say *dead*?" that can't be. I just talked to her last week.

"Yes. Well, two days after you told me you talked to Susan, they found her body in her apartment. They stated that they didn't know how long she had been there. Someone smelled an odor coming from her apartment and called the police. So you could not have talked to her when you said you did."

"But I did not only talk to her, I saw her too!"

"There must be some kind of mistake. I told the police that you had just talked to her a week ago, and they said that was impossible because she had been dead for some time."

Veronica, I wondered if I know this is the last minute and all, but I wondered if you would go to New York with me to claim Susan's body? You two were such good friends. We will be there for about a week. Do you think you can get away for a week?"

"Yes, I'll be happy too. I'll just let them know that I had a death in the family, and I have to go to New York for a couple of weeks. So there shouldn't be any problem.

"Thank you, Veronica, you were Susan's best friend. Thank you for considering going with me."

"Thank you for asking. I loved Susan, and I would do anything for her," I said.

I took the two weeks off, and Mrs. Brown and I went to New York. I still couldn't believe that Susan was dead. I had just talked to her on the phone. I wanted to take her business card to prove that I had seen her and talked to her. But I couldn't find that card anywhere. I thought I left it in my bag, but it wasn't there. That was alright, I knew Susan, and I had talked and that I had seen her. I was hoping it was a mistake that it wasn't Susan that they had found but someone else, that Susan was on vacation with her friend and would show up, and we would have a good laugh about this.

But when we got to New York, I knew it wasn't a mistake. I knew it was Susan they had founded. For some reason, I just knew it was her even before we went to the police station. I don't know; how I knew I just did, it was this kind of a strange feeling I got soon as we got off the plane. I looked at Mrs. Brown and started to cry.

"What is it, Veronica? What's the matter?" Mrs. Brown asked, drying the tears from my face.

I looked at Susan's mother with tears running down my face. I know that it's Susan. I know the way she looked when they found her. I also know how they found her. I mean, I know what shape she was in when they found her.

"How could you know that?" her mother asked.

"It's hard to explain; I just know," I said. We got a cab and went to the police station.

"Why does everything have to happen in New York?" Mrs. Brown wondered aloud as we made our way to the police station.

"I don't know, I said. I wish I would have been here for my blue eyes, friend."

You did use to call Susan that; when I first heard you say that, I was upset. Susan just laughed it off and said, "Get real, mom Ronnie doesn't mean anything bad by that." You know you were the only one she let call her that.

That's because we had a bond. I loved Susan, and Susan loved me. We were more than friends; we were, well, it's hard to explain, but it was as if we were one person, sometimes in two separate bodies.

When we got to the police station, we told them why we were there, and they asked us to wait. Someone will be with us shortly.

While we were waiting, I thought about all the fun Susan and I had together. The guys she wouldn't go out with unless they had a friend for me. I would tell her, "You will never get another date if you keep dragging me along."

Then we won't have dates together," she would say with a smile.

I remember when Carol Watson told everyone we were gay. Susan got so mad that she wanted to fight Carol.

Don't worry about it, I told her. People will believe what they want to believe regardless of what we say or do," I tried telling her. I always had to talked Susan out of fighting someone for something stupid they said about us.

I remember getting the flu and couldn't go to school for a week. Bobby called and told me about a fight she had gotten into one day.

"You should have seen her, Veronica," he said. (he never called me anything but Veronica) Belinda and Joan were coming down the hall, and she overheard them say something about you; she didn't do anything or say anything to them then, but after school, did she let Belinda have it. I tried to break it up before they both got put out of school.

Mr. Walker came out of the building; what's going on here? You know how he sounds.

"Ms. Brown and Ms. Mills, is there any trouble here?" he asked them.

"No," Belinda said, "I tripped, and Susan was helping me pick my books up.

"I see," he said. "Are you sure that what happened?" He asked her. (not believing a word she said)

"Yes," she said. Then she turned to Susan and said, "Thanks for helping me, Susan." Then she turned and walked away. That was that Bobby said, laughing.

Now my blue eyes friend, who was always trying to take up for me, was gone.

CHAPTER SEVEN

I sat there deep in thought, wondering what had happened to Susan over the years. Finally, I looked up, just in time to see the most handsome man I had ever seen. He was coming over to Mrs. Brown and me. "Mrs. Brown?" I'm Officer Jackson. I'm sorry for your loss.

"Thank you. I brought Susan's friend with me if that okay?" She said.

"That fine. I'll be taking you to the morgue in a couple of minutes," he told us.

"Thank you," Mrs. Brown said. She turned to me and said, "I don't think I can do this."

"Yes, you can. I'll be there with you; it'll be alright, I promise," I told her. Ten minutes later, we were on our way to the morgue.

Mrs. Brown stood there, holding my hand every tightly, trying not to cry. When we got to the morgue, she asked if it would be okay if I went in with her. We stood there looking down at Susan. I couldn't believe it was her. I remembered the last conversation we had. I turned to ask the officer when they had found Susan's body? And how long had she been dead?

"A couple of days ago. She had been dead for about two or three weeks," he said.

"That couldn't be right," I said.

"Why do you say that, miss?" He asked.

"Because I saw her, and she made plans to come and visit me last week. Remember, Mrs. Brown? I called, looking for her. Because she was in town, I saw her!"

"Oh? "When was this?" the officer asked.

"Last week, I was coming out of a restaurant when I ran into her," I told him.

"Are you sure it was her?" Officer Jackson asked.

"Of course, I'm sure she was my best friend. We even talk on the phone for a while. She said that things weren't going too well for her right now, and she needed someone to talk to. And I asked her if she had vacation time coming, and she said that she did, and I asked her to come for a visit, and she said she would and that she would call let me know when her flight got in," I said all in one breath.

"You couldn't have talked to her, miss," he said.

"Veronica, my name is Veronica Smith," I told him.

"You couldn't have talked to her; she was dead more than two weeks when we found her miss," he replied.

"I don't understand; if she was dead, how could I have talked to her?" I wonder out loud.

"I don't know, miss," he said.

Can you stop calling me that? My name is Veronica

"Can we leave now?" Mrs. Brown asked. I would like to make arrangements to take my daughter home.

"Yes, a course, but it will be a couple of days before we can release the body. Where are you staying?"

"I thought that maybe we could stay at Susan's?" Mrs. Brown told him.

"I don't think that will be possible. It's still a crime scene."

"Well, we didn't make any other arrangement," Mrs. Brown said.

"Let me call and see what I can do to get you a room, okay?" he asked.

"Fine, I guess we could wait at the station," I told Susan, mother.

Officer Jackson called and got us a room at one of the hotels not far from the station.

"Maybe I can come back when my shift end, and we can talk?"

"If you like," I said. Is that okay with you, Mrs. Brown?

"That's fine; I'm just going to make some calls and go to bed early. But, Veronica, you're old enough now to call me Gloria."

"If you think it will be alright."

"It's okay, dear," Mrs. Brown reassured me with a sad smile.

Thank you, Mrs. Brown, I mean Gloria.

That evening Officer Jackson came back and talked to Mrs. Brown about Susan. Would you like something to eat, or have you eaten already? He asked. No, thank you, Mrs. Brown said, I'm not hungry.

"But maybe Veronica could use something to eat. She hasn't eaten all day."

He turned to me and asked, "Would you like to get something to eat?"

"I don't want to leave Mrs. Brown alone," I said.

"That alright, dear, I'm going to make some calls and turn in early."

"Okay, if you think you will be alright. I just didn't want to leave you alone."

"You should go and try to enjoy yourself."

"Okay, if you think I should." I'll just get a jacket, "I shouldn't' belong," Veronica told Mrs. Brown as she went to get her jacket.

CHAPTER EIGHT

"Tell me, how do you know the victim?" Officer Jackson asked as soon as we got on the elevator.

"You mean Susan. We went to school together."

"Really?" he asked, sounding surprised.

"Why does that surprise you? We went from preschool through high school together."

"What kind of person was she?" he wanted to know.

"You would've liked her a lot if you had met her. She was so full of life, a great person to be around; we were always together. If not at her house, then at mine. People used to call us *the twins*. Some people couldn't understand why we hung around with each other. But we got along from the first time we met. I used to call Susan my blue eyes friend. No one could understand that. They thought that Susan should get angry at me for saying it, but they didn't realize it was a compliment. Not even our parents understood it. One day Susan's mother heard me call her my blue eyes friend and told me to go home. She said, "that it wasn't a very nice thing to say." But Susan understood that's why we got along so well together. You know some people weren't very happy with our friendship."

"Did Susan have any enemies that you could think of?" he asked.

"No, none that I know. You must remember I hadn't seemed Susan in years."

"How many years?" he wanted to know.

"About six. We stay in touch the first year out of college; then, we lost contact with each other about a year after that."

"But I thought you said you saw her about three weeks ago?"

I thought I had; but when I called Susan's mother to see if she was there, her mother said she hadn't seen or heard from her in weeks. But I could have sworn that I saw her outside a fast-food restaurant. And then there was the phone call. Susan and I talked for about two hours on the phone, and she said that she would spend two weeks with me because she had vacation time coming to her. After a week had passed and I hadn't heard from her I called her mother. That's when I found out she was dead."

"What did you talk about?" he asked.

"Who? Me and Susan?"

"Yes, what did you talk about?" he asked again.

"Her job, high school, old friends—-things like that."

"Why are you asking me all these questions?" I wanted to know.

"Just routine. I thought that I would save you a trip down to the station tomorrow."

"To the station? Why do I have to go down to the station?"

"Because you said you talked to her last week, so that makes you the last person to talk to her."

"Yes, but that was back in Chicago, where I live. I have never been to New York. You said she had been dead weeks before."

"You never been to New York? He asked.

"No, never."

"That's strange; how did you know she was dead?" he asked.

"I didn't. I thought that she was coming for a visit. So when she didn't call me or show up, I called her mother, and that is how I found out that Susan was dead."

"But you knew the way to her place. You even knew what floor she lived on, what apartment she lived in."

"I know that's why people thought we were strange because I knew things about Susan sometimes even before she did. It worked both ways; she knew things about me the same way."

"Oh, like ESP?' he asked.

"No, not exactly; it was something more than that. It's like that *twin* thing I was telling you about."

"What twin thing?" he wanted to know.

"You know the one where one *twin* knows what the other was thinking and feeling whether they were together or not."

"I heard about that, but you and Susan were not *twins;* you weren't even related."

"I know that's why people thought we were so strange."

"Let me tell you about the day I saw Susan. I was having kind of an odd day. You see, I woke up and saw all this blood over everything in my apartment. I didn't know what had happened. I didn't know how it got there. So I went to the police station to report it. They thought I was crazy. They sent an investigation team to check it out. But when they got back to my apartment, everything had been cleaned up."

"Cleaned up? There was nothing there? They found nothing at all," he asked

"Yes, that's just what I mean. There wasn't any blood anywhere."

"Did you clean it up while you waited for the police?"

"No, I stayed at the station to wait and went back with them."

"What did they say when they found the place clean?"

"I told you they thought I was crazy. Accused me of filing a false report."

"Did they look around or anything?"

"Yes, in fact, they use that blue light to look for blood and couldn't find any. After the police had left, I thought about going to work, but I didn't. I went to this fast food place for some lunch. When I looked at my watch, two hours had passed. I got up to leave, and that's when I bumped into Susan. I was coming out the door and wasn't looking where I was going when we bumped into one another. The funny thing is I didn't recognize her. We stood there talking, and all the time, I was trying to figure out who she was."

"You couldn't remember her?"

"No. I didn't know who she was until I looked at the card she had given me. Then I remembered, and everything came rushing back. I couldn't wait to talk to her."

"You said she was your best friend that you grew up together, and you couldn't remember her?"

"I know it was strange to me too. It was because something was different about the way she looked. She didn't look quite like herself. After she had walked away, I looked at the card she had given me. But then, I remember her right away. She even called me that night on the phone. We talked for an hour or two, maybe longer."

"What did you talk about?" he wanted to know

"I told you about kids we went to school with and about how long it had been since we seem one another. I remember we talked about this boy named Bobby, who went to school with us and about Carol Watson and some of the other kids we knew."

"Is that all?"

"No, she started telling me about a guy she had met through her firm. How she had run into him one day at Bloomingdale."

"Oh, what happened?" he asked.

"She said he was there with his wife, and she walked up to him and kissed him and called him darling.

She said he got so angry because his wife was there and that she didn't know he was married. She said he can over to her apartment a couple of nights later and asked why she had done it in front of his wife? Susan said she asked him why he didn't tell her he was married. She told him that she thought they would get married one day. He asked her what gave her the idea that he would marry her. She said I thought you loved me? Then she told me things started to change at her job. She wasn't getting the clients she used to get anymore.

Some of her old clients were taken away from her, and she didn't know why. Susan said one night he came by, and she asked him if he had anything to do with it. Was he the reason she wasn't getting any more work?"

"And what did he say?"

"He didn't know what she was talking about."

"Did she tell you his name?"

"No, and I didn't ask."

"Is that all you talk about?"

"Yes, except she was crying, and that when I asked her to come for a visit, and she said she would. That she would call me with the flight number and the time of her arrival."

"And you didn't talk to her anymore after that?"

"No, I thought it was strange for her to say she would call me with her arrival time when I had just seemed her. I did call her mother to see if she was there, but her mother said she hadn't heard from her in weeks. I wondered what was going on, but I figured she would explain when I saw her. A week went by, and I still hadn't heard from Susan, and I called her mother and that when I found out, Susan was dead. My blue eyes friend was gone. I still can't understand why I didn't recognize her."

"You didn't recognize her when you first saw her?"

"I told you before, not at first. I mean, it had been years since the last time I saw her. And she had changed".

"Change, what do you mean that she had changed?"

"I don't know, really, just little things."

"Such as?"

"Her hair was shorter; she had on a little too much makeup; her clothes weren't fitting her right. You know, little things like that."

"And you notice those things in the short time the two of you talked?"

"Yes, it like I said, Susan, and I notices things like that about each other. It was like when Mrs. Brown and I got off the plane. I knew immediately that it was Susan who was found dead. It was just a feeling I got." I was hoping it wasn't true, but it was.

"So you and Susan were that close?"

"Yes, can we talk about something else?"

"Okay, let's talk about you. Tell me what Veronica Smith is like?"

CHAPTER NINE

"I'm an average person. I work, come home, cook, watch TV, and go to bed," I told him.

"What do you do for fun?" he asked me.

"Go to the movies sometimes."

"Is that all?" he asked.

"Yes," I said.

"What about your family? Your parents, are they still living?"

"No, my parents died a year ago in a car accident."

"No sisters or brothers?"

"No, I told you I was an only child."

"Yes, you did. I forgot."

"Did you? Or were you trying to trick me?"

"No, I did forget that you said you were an only child. Let's talk about something else, okay?"

"I know, let's talk about you," I said.

"Okay, what do you want to know?"

"Well, let's see. Mum, what's your first name?"

"Cleophus."

"Cleophus? I thought it would be John or William or something like that."

"No, just plain Cleophus Jackson. No middle name."

"No middle name, why?"

"Does it matter?" he asked.

"No, I just thought that you would have a middle name. So what do your friends call you, Cleo?"

"No, most people call me Jackson or Jack."

"And you let them?"

"Why not? What would you call me if we were friends?"

"Well, I don't know; let me think about it."

"While you are thinking, tell me, what do your friends call you? Let me guess, Ronnie, right?"

"No, people call me Veronica, the only person that ever called me Ronnie was Susan."

"Your parents never called you, Ronnie?" he asked

"No, they said if they had wanted to call me Ronnie, they would have named me Ronnie. They haven't named me Ronnie. Therefore, my name was Veronica, and that was what I was to be called. They didn't like the idea of people shorten their name, nor did they like nicknames for that matter."

"So how did Susan get away with calling you, Ronnie," he said with a smile

"She didn't at first. I remember the first time she did. I guess we were about four, and my mother came to school to pick me up, and Susan said I'll see you tomorrow Ronnie."

My mother liked to have a fit. So when we got home, she said, "What did that little girl mean by calling you, Ronnie Veronica?" Didn't you tell her your name was Veronica? "Yes, mommy," I said, but she said I didn't look like a Veronica to her, so she would call me Ronnie. She said Ronnie was better.

I don't care what sounds better to her. Your name is Veronica, and if she can't call you that, you cannot play with her. When you go to school tomorrow, tell her your mother said she is to call you Veronica and not Ronnie."

"Yes, mommy," I said. But when I got to school the next day, Susan said, "I'm sorry your mommy will not let me call you Ronnie, but you just don't look like a Veronica to me. Maybe I could call you Ronnie when she is not around."

"How did you know my mommy didn't want you calling me Ronnie?" I asked her.

"I don't know; maybe I heard her telling you to tell me your name was Veronica and not Ronnie." But we had been at home when my mother told me to tell Susan she couldn't call me Ronnie.

I wondered about it, but then it slipped my mind as things do when you are a child. I didn't think any more about it until we were in the fifth grade, and Susan did it again, called me Ronnie in front of my mother. The strange thing is my mother didn't say anything about it.

"Maybe it didn't matter anymore to your mother."

Yes, it matter. Susan was the only person my mother would accept, calling me Ronnie. She wouldn't let anyone else call me anything but Veronica until the day she died. I couldn't understand why maybe because she could see how close Susan and I were becoming.

"Was Susan your only friend?" he asked.

"No, I had pleasantly of friends; it's just Susan, and I was very close. We were closer than most sisters."

"Have you thought about what you might call me yet?"

"No, not yet, it will come to me. "This is a beautiful place."

"I thought you might like it."

"I do; it feels friendly. It's like you sitting in a friend's living room."

"I'm glad you like it. Tell me some more about you and Susan."

"There not much more to tell. After Susan and I returned from Hawaii, we went to different colleges.

We stay in touch. We would visit each other at our various schools. Sometimes it was fun, and sometimes it wasn't."

"Oh, why was that?" he asked.

"Oh, because Susan went to a white college and I went to a black one. Well, it did have a few whites there. Anyway, when I went to visit Susan, her friends would give me a hard time."

"Because of that *twin* thing?"

"Yes, maybe in a way I don't know. When I visited Susan, it was this one girl who just wouldn't leave me alone. It's seen everywhere we went she was there calling me Susan, little *nigger* friend or spooky or something else just as bad. There was this party Susan took me to, and she was there. Boy, did she start in on me? I tried to get Susan to leave, but she wouldn't; she said I had just as much right to be there as she did. Her name was Clara. Mum, I just remember that.

Well, anyway, Susan turned to me, and we looked at each other, don't I said, and she said, "Oh yes, maybe this will teach her a lesson."

We said all that without saying a word out loud. I said, "wait, let's see if she stops."

But she didn't as the even went on; she only got worse.

"Okay," I said, let do it.

"Do what?" he wanted to know.

"Well, sometimes we could put things into people's minds just by thinking it."

"So, what did the two of you do?"

"Susan started," I said.

"Started what?" he asked.

Whenever Clara would try and say something negative about me, Susan would make it come out positive. Clara started to say something about my hair to one of her friends, and Susan made it come out; doesn't Susan's friend Veronica have beautiful hair? I wish I could do that with my hair. She started to say how tacky my clothes were, and we made her say I love Veronica's outfit. I wonder where she got it? That is the closeness we share. I'm really going to miss her.

"Didn't you say you hadn't seen her for a while?" he asked.

"Yes, but just knowing she was, there was enough."

That enough about Susan. Tell me something about yourself.

"Do you have any brothers or sisters?" I asked him.

"I have two brothers and one sister."

What are their names?

"Marcus, Charles, and Jean, my brother Marcus is the oldest."

"You must be the youngest of the four."

"No, that my sister Jean she the baby."

"Are your parents still living?"

"No, they died when I was a boy."

"I'm sorry to hear that."

"Thanks, but you don't have to be sorry. I hardly remember them. I was young when they died."

"What happened to them, if you don't mind me asking?"

"No, I don't mind. My parents died in a fishing accident. My parents love to fish, so they decided to go on a fishing trip to Michigan, and the boat they were using got in trouble, and they were too far out to make it back to shore, so they drowned. My mother couldn't swim, and my father refused to leave her. So they died together."

"I'm so very sorry. It must have been hard for you and your brothers and sister."

"I guess it was at the time; as I said, I don't remember most of what happened; I was too young."

"Are you and your family close?" I asked him.

"Yes, if it wasn't for Marcus, I don't know what we would have done. He kept the family together when the state wanted to put us in foster care. If it weren't for him, I wouldn't be a cop today."

Police officer.

"What?" he asked

"A police officer, not a cop. You said cop, and you are not a cop; you are a police officer. I'm not too fond of the word cop. It's a bad word to me."

"Why do you say that?"

"Do you know what the word cop stands for?" I asked him.

"No, what?"

"Criminal On Patrol. I don't like that, so, therefore, you are not a cop."

"You are a strange person Veronica Smith, and I would like to get to know you better. My family would just love you."

"How do you know? They may think I'm as strange as you think I am."

"I don't think you strange in a strange way. I just meant you don't think like other people, and you take things differently for everyone else."

"I thought we were going to talk about you for a while?"

"I'm sorry I didn't mean to get you upset; it's just that there's something about you that I like and would like to know more about the real you."

"This is the real me. No ups, no extras. Just me, plain old Veronica Marie Smith."

"Yours not old, and believe me, you are not plain."

"Can we talk about something else, please?"

"You don't like talking about yourself, do you?"

"No, because there is nothing to talk about. I would like to hear more about your family, but it's getting late, and we have a lot to do in the morning."

"Oh, you want to go?"

"Please, I know I'm not very good company, and I'm really tired if you don't mind?"

"Okay, I'll take you back to the hotel."

CHAPTER TEN

Good morning Sergeant. Morning Jackson "How did things go last night with that Smith woman? Was she the last one to see this Susan Brown alive?"

"Yes and no."

"What do you mean, yes and no? Was she or wasn't she the last to see Ms. Brown alive?"

"That just it, sergeant she thought she saw her back in Chicago, but at the time she saw her, Ms. Brown was already dead."

"What do you mean she was already dead?"

"Remember the coroner said Ms. Brown had been dead about two weeks? Veronica says she saw her coming out of a restaurant in Chicago on that same day."

"It's Veronica, is it?"

She asked me to call her by her first name. She doesn't like being called by her last name.

How could she have seemed her on the same day? The sergeant asked.

I don't know, but she can describe the room we found her friend in if you talk to her. She said she woke up that morning covered with blood, took a shower, went to the police station, and reported it.

Did the cops check it out?

The police officers did and couldn't find a thing. They told her she must have dreamt it, after that she saw her friend.

We better call Chicago and check out her story. Hey, Knight, I want you to call Chicago and check out a story that Ms. Veronica Smith told the police there and get back to me.

A couple of hours later, Officer Knights came back with the report. Her story checks out serge they said, they went over her apartment with a fine-tooth comb and couldn't find a thing, and there no way anyone could have clean that apartment as clean as it was in the time it took them to get to it. Said they check her out too.

Only child's parents died a few years back. She is shy, get along with all her co-works, stays to herself, no close friend. She was the same way in school and only had one close friend, Susan Brown, who moved to New York. Could that be the Brown we found in the apartment?

I want you to get a picture of Ms. Smith, show it around, and see if she ever visited her friend here. Start at her apartment and then her job. I want you and Jackson to work on this. I like some answers before she leaves the city.

"Well, we better get started; they plan to make arrangements and leave as soon as possible," Officer Jackson said.

"Is this her?" Knight asked Jackson.

"Yes, that her beautiful girl, isn't she?" But she doesn't think so.

"Well, let's get started," Officer Knight said.

They took Veronica's picture to Susan's job, but no one there had ever seemed her before. Next, they went to Susan apartment, and the doorman man said the first time he ever saw her was when she came into town with Susan's mother. They were on their way out when Veronica and Susan's mother got off the elevator.

"What are you doing here?" Veronica asked.

"We were just asking the doorman a few questions," Officer Knight replied.

"Oh, I thought you were checking to see if I've been here before."

"Why would you think that?" Officer Knight asked.

"Because Susan been dead for three weeks and the first thing you would do is see if she had any outside visitor. You will have told the doorman that if he sees anyone he recognizes to give you a call. Isn't that right?"

"Well, what did he tell you? Had he seen me before?"

"As a matter of fact, no, he said he saw you for the first time when you came in with Ms. Brown's mother. He said he would have remembered someone like you."

"What does he mean someone like me? I'm just like everyone else."

"You far from being like everyone else. Don't you know how you look? You're a beautiful young woman." Officer Knight told her.

"No, I'm not. I'm just plain old Veronica Smith." Let's go, Gloria, excuse us; we have to arrange for my friend to be taken back home to Chicago."

Office Jackson and Knight watched as Veronica and Mrs. Brown left the hotel.

"I told you she doesn't think of herself as being beautiful."

"Well, be that as it may, she's a stunning young lady," Officer Knight said.

"I thought you told me you didn't look at a black woman like that?" Officer Jackson asked him.

"For her, I'll make an acceptance. Come on, let's check out Ms. Brown's place of employment again."

CHAPTER ELEVEN

We went to the morgue to ask when we could take Susan home. They told us it would be a couple of days. So we decide to stop for lunch. We were at a sidewalk café. I looked up and thought I saw Susan across the street just standing there looking at her mother and me. I know that couldn't be true, haven't we just left her body at the morgue? Wasn't the police investigating her death? What was going on? I couldn't understand.

Mrs. Brown was saying something to me; she was calling my name. "Veronica? Veronica! "Are you alright?"

"Yes, fine." Sorry, I didn't hear what you were saying.

"Who were you looking at across the street?"

"No one I thought I saw, but that couldn't be."

"You thought you saw whom?"

"No one, what were you saying?" I asked

"I said I was going back to the hotel. I still had a couple of calls to make."

"That fine. I think I'll stay here a little while longer, if that okay?"

"That will be fine," Mrs. Brown said.

"Are you sure you'll be okay?" she asked.

"Yes, maybe I'll do a little shopping."

I sat there looking across the street. I couldn't believe I saw what I thought I saw. I don't know how long I sat there. I got up to leave when my cell phone started to ring. Who could be calling me? The only people I knew were back in Chicago.

"Hello, Ronnie, how are you doing? I saw you having lunch with my mother."

"Susan? Susan, is this you?" No, it couldn't be you're dead. Your body is in the morgue.

"Ronnie, I need your help."

"How are you calling me? Where are you? Are you trying to drive me crazy?"

"No, Ronnie. I need your help."

"My help? Why? Help for what?"

"To catch the people who kill me."

"Did I see you back in Chicago? Was it you I talked to on the phone when I got home that day? Is it you now?"

"Yes, I need your help."

This cannot be happening. Oh, God, what am I going to do? If I tell someone, they will think I'm nuts.

"Ronnie, are you listening to me?"

"Oh my God, what am I going to do?"

"Ronnie?"

Maybe I am crazy.

"Veronica, listen to me."

That got my attention. Susan only called me Veronica when there was something important she needed to tell me.

"I'm listening. What is it you want, Susan?"

"That better. Now, remember when I told you about the man I was seeing? Well, his wife found out he was cheating on her with me. She found out about the apartment and everything and came over to see me. We talked, I thought she knew about what was going on between me and her husband but I was wrong. She didn't know. She was just trying to figure out what was happening between her husband and me. I tried to convince her that nothing was going on, but she didn't believe me. We talked for about an hour. I thought everything was alright when she left. At least I wanted it to be alright. So I made myself believe it."

"So, what happened?"

"John came over a couple of days later and accused me of telling her everything. I tried to convince him I hadn't, but he didn't believe me. I was so afraid I didn't know what he would do. I've never seem him that angry before. I tried talking to him. I told him I hadn't told her a thing. He just looked at me for the longest of time, then he just left."

My phone was going out. "Susan, John, who?"

I couldn't hear her; my phone had cut out. What was I going to do? Who could I call? Who would believe me? I could tell Mrs. Brown what had happened. No, she wouldn't believe me. I could go to the police. No, they would only think I was a nut. I didn't know what to do.

I don't know how long I sat there. I didn't know what to do or think. I was about to leave when Officer Jackson came up to me.

"What are you doing here? Are you following me?" I asked him.

"No, Mrs. Brown told me this is where she left you a couple of hours ago. Why are you still here?"

"I was just about to leave when you came up. Why were you looking for me? You found out something about Susan?"

"No, I just wanted to know if you would like to have dinner with me tonight."

"I don't know; it didn't go too well last night."

"I promise not to talk about the case tonight if you come out with me."

I don't know. I said, looking everywhere to avoid looking in his eyes.

"Please?" he asked again.

"Well, okay, what time?"

"About seven-thirty, I'll pick you up down in the lobby."

"No, if you want to have dinner with me, you'll have to pick me up in my room or at the door, at least. I know that sounds old fashion, but my parents taught me if a young man was genuinely interested in seeing me, he could pick me up at my door."

"That's fine; I'll see you about seven-thirty then."

We got up to leave; he went to his squad car. I started walking down the street, still thinking about the strange afternoon I just had. (I didn't notice the man that was following me.)

CHAPTER TWELVE

When I got back to the room, Susan's mother was still on the phone. She hung up and told me Officer Jackson had been looking for me.

"I saw him. He came by the restaurant."

"You were still there?" she asked in amazement.

"Yes, I was thinking about something that had happened when he came up."

"Oh, what?"

"I thought I saw… never mind."

"You thought you saw what?"

"Nothing. Office Jackson asked me out to dinner again tonight if that's okay."

"That fine. I was thinking about going to bed early again this evening. My sister will be here in the morning."

"Are you sure you don't want me to stay here with you tonight? I did go out last night with Officer Jackson. I could stay in?"

"No, you go have dinner with that nice young man. I'll be fine like I said, my sister will be here tomorrow. I love my sister, but spending time with her isn't one of my favorite things to do. But she is my sister and Susan's aunt."

"She never did understand the relationship Susan, and I had, did she?"

"No, she didn't. Veronica, I'll try to keep her from upsetting you as much as I can. Maybe, she and I could do a little shopping tomorrow. I hope that will help. I'm sorry I asked her not to come, but she insisted."

"That's okay, Mrs. Brown. She is Susan's aunt, and it's only right you have a member of your family here with you at this time. I'll try to stay out of her way."

"Gloria, remember I asked you to call me Gloria."

"You know that very hard to do after calling you Mrs. Brown all these years."

"You're such a good person, Veronica. Now I understand my Susan loved and trusted you all these years."

"I loved her too. She was like the sister I never had. Well, if I'm going out, I better go get ready."

I left to get ready. I took my shower, but I didn't know what to do with my hair. See, it was very long people thought I had a weave in it, but I didn't. I tried telling them it was all mine. But they didn't believe me, so I stopped trying.

I usually wore it in a French roll or twist upon my head, but I didn't feel like taking the time to do it tonight. So I left it down. Well, here go nothing, I said to myself. I walk out to see what Gloria thought about me, leaving it down.

"Well, what do you think?" I asked, not knowing Gloria had left the room.

"I think it looks beautiful."

I looked up to see Officer Jackson standing there. "You look beautiful," he said.

"I didn't know you were here. I didn't hear you knock. "Where, Gloria?"

She said to tell you that she'll see you in the morning.

"Shall we go?" he asked

"Maybe I should just let her know I'm on my way out."

I knock on Mrs. Brown's door. Mrs. Brown, I mean, Gloria, I'm on my way out. I don't believe I'll be out last." (It's was something my parents taught me never to leave unless someone knew where I was going.)

"That fine. Go and have fun, and Veronica, your hair looks lovely like that. I didn't know you had so much of it. You looked beautiful like that."

"Thank you. I won't be too late."Veronica told her.

Office Jackson looked at me very strangely as we got in the elevator.

"Why are you staring at me like that?" I asked him.

"I've never seemed anyone as beautiful as you."

"Thank you. Do you think I should've worn my hair up?"

"Why? It looks just fine as it is," he said.

"I thought about cutting it," I said.

"Why would you want to do that?" he wanted to know.

"Because it too long to do anything with."

"I know what I like to do with it," he said,

"Excuse me?"

"Nothing, I was just thinking out loud," he said.

"So, where should we go?" I asked.

"Where would you like to go?"

"I don't know. I've never been here before, as I told you."

"Oh, yes, I forgot."

"Did you?" I asked him.

"Did I what?"

"Forget, or were you testing me again? Is this the way the evening going to be? If so, please take me back to the hotel."

"Yours so polite, but no, the evening is not going to be about me trying to get information out of you. I just forgot that all."

"Okay, so where are we going?"

"I know this place you're going to love it. I know the owner."

"Well, Let's go," I said.

(He wouldn't stop looking at me. I was so self-conscious. I kept touching my hair.)

"Are you sure I look okay for this place? You never told me what kind of place we were going to."

"You look beautiful. The owner will just love you." He took me to the most fascinating, place I've been to in a long time.

"Do you like it?" he asked.

"Yes, it's a beautiful place," I said.

"What would you like?"

"Why don't you order for me?"

He placed our order. While we were waiting, a charming young lady came to the table. She looked sort of familiar to me. Like I should know her. But that was impossible. I have never been to New York before. I sat there quietly while she and Officer Jackson greeted each other. Then he introduces me to her, "this is my sister Jean. Jean, this is Veronica Smith, the girl I was telling you about."

That's why she looked so familiar; she was his sister. She smiled, hello. Hello, I said I thought you looked like someone I knew. You have a very charming place.

"Thank you, CJ told me all about you," she said.

How could he? I thought I just met him yesterday.

"CJ, is that what you call him?" I asked.

"Yes, some of my friends started calling him that when he would come to visit me in school, and it stuck."

"What do you call him?"

"Officer Jackson, I don't know him that well," I told her.

"You're right. I do like her. Your dinner will be up shortly." She said as she left the table.

"Your sister seems to be very nice, but you should've told me you were bringing me to meet her."

"Why? Was it a problem?" he asks.

"No, but I could've fixed my hair differently. What must she think of me looking like this?" I said, touching my hair.

"Like what?" he asked.

"I don't know, so unkempt."

"You look beautiful, breathtaking."

CHAPTER THIRTEEN

Dinner arrived, so I chose not to answer him. While we were eating, I was wondering should I tell him what had happened today. I was so deep in thought I didn't see his sister had returned.

"How was everything?" she asked.

"Wonderful, I never tasted anything so good," I told her.

"Thanks, glad you enjoy it. Would you like some dessert?"

"No, thanks, just coffee, please, if that all right with you, Officer Jackson?"

"That find," he said.

Jean left to get the coffee.

"Why do you call me Officer Jackson? I'm not on duty now."

"I don't know. What should I call you then?"

"How about Jacks?"

"No, that a child game. Not a name for someone like you." I said. "No, I think I'll call you CJ if that's alright?"

"Yes, I think that will be all right."

"Do you think your sister will object?"

"No, she'll be okay with it."

"I like your sister. She reminds me of someone I once knew."

"Who?" He asked.

Jean came back to check on us one last time. "So, how was everything?" She asked again.

"Everything was wonderful. You have a wonderful place here. It's decorated very elegantly. The atmosphere is so warm and friendly."

"I do like her CJ; she's a keeper. And it will be alright if you call him CJ. I don't mind now; I won't be the only one to call him that."

Officer Jackson looked from his sister to Veronica. "Jean, how did you know she wanted to call me CJ?"

"I must've heard her asking you if it was okay with me when I was coming to the table. Will you come back to visit soon?"

"The next time I get to New York, I'll come to visit you, I promise," I told her

"Are you ready to go?" Officer Jackson asked as he stood up.

"Yes, I got to get up early in the morning."

"Why do you have to get up so early?" he asked.

"Mrs. Brown's sister is coming in tomorrow to help with the funeral arrangement."

"You know they're not releasing the body until Friday; that's in two days. So what will you do until then?

"I don't know help Gloria as must as I can, I guess. I don't get along with Susan's aunt. She never liked me. I asked Susan about it once, and she said, "Don't worry about it; she said her aunt didn't like a lot of people. I'm really going to miss her. I know it was years since we saw one another, but as long as she was here, I could call her. I knew things would be alright."

"Well, here we are. Thank you for dinner; your sister was nice. I like her."

"I would like to see you again before you leave, if that's possible?"

"I don't know; maybe I have to think about it. I'll call you at the station if I decide to see you, okay?"

"I guess it has to be."

CHAPTER FOURTEEN

When I got back to the room, a message was waiting for me. It was from someone named Felecia. The note said she would give me a call in the morning. Gloria was in bed, so I couldn't ask her who this person was.

Mrs. Brown was already up and dressed when I finally got up the next morning. "Good morning, dear. How was the evening?"

"It was fun. I found the note you left me last night. Who is Felecia?"

"I don't know said she worked with Susan."

"Why would she want to talk to me when she could have spoken to you?"

"I don't know. She said that she would call you this morning."

"Did she tell you what time?"

"No, just that she needed to talk to you."

"Well, I hope she calls before we have to leave to go and pick your sister up from the airport."

"You go to the airport? With me, why?"

"Yes, don't you want me to go with you to pick up your sister?"

"No, I can go by myself. You can stay and wait for the call from Felecia."

"I wonder why she didn't tell you what she wanted."

"I don't know, all she said was she had tried to reach you at home and couldn't, and then she called your job and found out you were here.

"I don't know who she is. You did say she said she worked with Susan." How did she know to call my home? How did she get my number? Who would've given it to her? I wonder to myself.

"Well, maybe I'll stay here and wait for her call to see what this is all about. I told Mrs. Brown.

Gloria went to prepare herself to meet her sister's plane while I waited for Felecia to call. She called about five minutes after Gloria left.

"Hello, to whom am I speaking?"

"Veronica Smith."

"Good, my name is Felecia Jordan. I used to work with Susan."

"Yes, go on."

"Susan told me a lot about you, and I just wanted to talk to you about her if you feel up to it."

"Why?" Do you know something about who might have killed her? If so, you should go to the police and tell them what you know."

"Well, it not so much that I know something; it's just well. I need to talk to you if that okay?" Felecia said.

"I guess so. Can you at least tell me what this is about?"

"I will when I see you, alright?"

"When do you want to meet?" I asked her.

How about lunch?

"That will be all right," I said.

"Where should we go? She asked me.

"I don't know this is my first time coming to New York, but I do know this place where I had dinner last night; the food was excellent."

"Okay, do you know if it's open for lunch?"

"I think so; I'm not sure. If not, we can go somewhere else."

So we met at Jean's restaurant for lunch. I got there first and asked to be seated close to the door as possible. I never did like meeting strangers in public places. I know that's strange, but I get nervous when talking to new people. I saw her as she came through the door. She seemed to recognize me the minute she walked in, which was a disadvantage for me. I thought maybe I would have time to study her before we met. But it was not to be. So I prepare myself for what I might hear. She was blond like Susan, but that's where the resemblance ends. She was not as pretty, kind of plain-looking.

"Veronica?"

"Yes?"

I'm Felecia, Felecia Jordan, a friend of Susan's. We worked at the same firm. I'm delighted to meet you at last. May, you look just like Susan described you.

"Is that good or bad? I know Susan would never say anything bad about me. But I don't know about you. Do you think Susan was right about me?"

"Yes, and you're right. Susan never did say anything bad about you. She was always Veronica this and Veronica that, and I had to meet you to see if everything she said was true."

"Is that why you wanted to have lunch with me to see if what she said about me was true?"

"No, it's just well it seemed impossible for anyone to be the way Susan told me you were."

"Were you and Susan close friends?" I asked her.

"Well, not close, but we did talk a lot."

"How was Susan the last time you saw her?" I asked.

"The last time I saw her, she was talking about maybe going home for a visit. She said things weren't going well right now, and she needed a break. You see, we work for the same firm but in a different department. I liked Susan a lot. I was sorry to hear about her death. I wish I had known her before she moves here."

Yes, she was quite a person. I loved her very much. Felecia looked at me. No, not like that, like a sister, we were close friends since we were children."

"Oh, really? I mean, she was white, and you are black."

"So, what has that to do with anything?"

"What did your parents think of that?"

"Everyone thought it was strange at first, but then they understood it."

"Understood it?" she asked, puzzle

"From the day we first met, it was as if we were meant to be best friends."

"Would you like to order now?" I looked up to see Jean standing there. She had such a strange look on her face.

"Yes, Felecia said I'll have a half tuna sandwich and a side salad. Veronica, what will you have?"

"A chef salad, I guess, and a glass of ice tea."

"It will be right up." Jean left, and I wondered what was on her mind to make her look at me like that.

CHAPTER FIFTEEN

"How well did you know Susan?" I asked Felecia. "Will I meet Susan a couple of years ago when I came to work for the firm. We seemed to hit it off, so we became friends. Oh, not like you two were friends, but friends. We would go out together sometime."

I looked at her as she talked. She was blond, like Susan was, with gray eyes not as pretty as Susan. We went out together sometimes, she was saying.

"Together?" I asked.

"Yes, why?" she asked.

"You don't look like the kind person Susan would've hung around."

"Why do you say that?"

"Because I knew Susan. And you don't seem like the kind of person she would hang out with."

"Will we did. We would meet after work and go to one club or another."

"I like Susan a lot. She was a good person."

"I know, Susan, and I would talk on the phone for hours when we were growing up."

"Did you and Susan talk much?" I asked her.

"Yes, but not as much as you and she talked."

"I didn't talk to Susan much these last few years; we kind of lost touch if you can believe that."

"Why, what happened?"

"You know the usual,—she was busy with work, and I was busy trying to start a business."

"Oh, what kind of business?"

I do parties and special events. I love to cook and arrange things; people are always trying to get me to do parties for them. I would call Susan, or she would call me, but we would just miss each other. I thought I saw her a few weeks ago outside a restaurant back home."

"How could that be? Wasn't she already dead by then?"

"How do you know that?" I asked her.

"I heard it around the office," she said.

"Around the office?"

I was about to ask her something else when Jean arrived with the food. She stayed and talked for a few minutes.

"How did the rest of the evening go last night, Ronnie?"

"It went fine. I like your brother."

"He liked you too. Can you see me before you leave?"

"Okay, is there something wrong?"

"No, I just like to talk to you before you go, if that's okay."

"That's fine. I'll see you before I leave," I said, turning back to Felecia.

"Did you know the man Susan was seeing?" I asked.

"Susan was seeing someone? I didn't know that," she said.

"I thought you said that you and she were friends."

"We were, but she didn't tell me everything."

"Was Susan happy here?" I asked her.

"What do you mean happy? How could she not be? She was young, blond, and beautiful living in New York; what else could she have possibly wanted?"

"I don't know, maybe a little love to go with everything else. Susan was a person with so much love to give, and she would've given it freely to the right person. Like she used to say," Ronnie, it takes more than looks to make it in this world." We sat there and ate in silence.

"About fifteen minutes later, Jean came over. "How is everything?" She asked.

"Everything is wonderful," Felecia said.

"Would you like some dessert?" Jean asked us.

"That sounds fine," Felecia said.

"What would you like?"

"What do you suggest?"

"We have about everything you can think of; you named it, we got it."

"Well, let's see. I would like to have a slice of white chocolate cake," Felecia said.

"Okay, and what would you like, Veronica?" Jean asked me.

"White chocolate sounds good," I said.

"I'll be back in a moment with your desert."

CHAPTER SIXTEEN

"Would you look at the time I got to get back to the office. Do you think she'll mind wrapping it up to go?"

"I don't believe so; just ask her when she comes back."

The waitress returned and said she would wrap it to go for Felecia. She stood up to leave.

"Well, it was nice meeting you, Veronica. You're everything Susan said you were. I hope we get to see each other again before you go back home. Do you know when that will be?"

"In a couple of days, I guess," I told her.

"Maybe I will see you before you leave; if not, have a safe trip back home."

"Thank you, and it was nice meeting you too."

Felecia left. I sit there thinking about the things she said and the things she didn't say, and something didn't feel right. Then it hit me—- she knew who had killed Susan. She was just trying to find out how much I knew.

I sat there for I don't know how long. I hadn't noticed that Jean had came over. "Are you alright?"

"Yes, I'm fine. It's just that lady I was talking with; I just got the strangest feeling about her."

"What kind of feeling?"

"It's hard to explain; I got the sense that she knows who killed Susan or at least something about it."

"So, what are you going to do?"

"I don't know; think about it for a while, I guess."

"Don't you think you should tell my brother about this?"

"No, maybe it's nothing. Let me think about it, and if I feel he should know, then I will tell him."

"Are you going to see him tonight?"

"No, I don't think I should."

"Why not?"

"Because I've seen him every night since I've been here."

"So what? I think he likes you a lot."

"How could he? He doesn't even know me. Besides, I'll be going home in a couple of days, and he'll never see me again."

"Are you sure about that?"

"Yes, I am beside; why would he want to see me after this is over?"

"Because he thinks you are an extraordinary person."

"But I'm not. Just look at me. Why would anyone in their right mind think I'm special?"

"What are you talking about? You are a gorgeous woman, and any man would be honored to see you again."

"If you say so, I got to go. Maybe, I'll see you again before I leave the city."

"I hope so. I think we could be good friends."

"I do too."

CHAPTER SEVENTEEN

I got up to leave and couldn't stop thinking about Felecia Jordan and what she had said. It wasn't so much what she said but the way she said it. When I got back to the hotel, Gloria was there with her sister.

"Hello Veronica, you remember my sister?"

"Yes, it's nice to see you again."

"Nice to see you too. Gloria was telling me you thought you saw Susan the day she died."

"Yes, I guess it wasn't her."

"How could you make a mistake like that? Then you had the nerve to call my sister and ask for her."

"Melissa, that enough, so she called and asked to speak to Susan; that was before we even knew she was dead. If it hadn't been for Veronica, I wouldn't be able to go through all I've been through. So leave her alone. She was a good friend to Susan."

"If you say so, I never could understand why Susan wanted to be around her or why you let her for that matter."

"That enough, if I had known this was the way you would behave, I would have told you to stay at home. Veronica had been such a big help to me, and I will not have you treating her this way."

"That's alright, Gloria; I'm going to my room. I have a lot to think about."

"Gloria? Gloria, when did you start calling her by her first name?"

"Melissa, that enough. I told Veronica to call me Gloria. She's an adult, and I don't have a problem with it."

"That's okay, Gloria. If it makes your sister feel better, if I call you Mrs. Brown, then I'll call you that."

"Melissa, I will not have you behaving that way with Veronica. She was Susan's best friend."

"And I still don't know why you let Susan be friend with her."

"I didn't either at first, but then Susan and Veronica had a friendship that I couldn't explain; it was like they were a part of one another. Knowing what the other was thinking like, they could read each other minds—better friends than we're sisters. So when Susan was unhappy, Veronica knew what to do to cheer her up. She was here to help me when you didn't have time to come to New York with me."

"I couldn't get time off from my job."

"Did you even ask Melissa? Did you even try to get the time off?"

"Will, no, I thought, you could handle it. and if you needed me, you would've of call, but you didn't, so that why I called you."

"I didn't need you because Veronica was here. She took time off with no problem. All I did was asked, and she said okay and took time off. So I will not have you treat Veronica like she's unimportant because she is to me. If you can't respect that, then you can go back home on the next plane."

CHAPTER EIGHTEEN

I was sitting in my room. Hearing but not wanting to listen to what was going on in the next room. My thoughts turn to the luncheon I had with Felecia Jordan, thinking about not what she said but what she didn't say. I was sitting there thinking when the phone started to ring. I thought Mrs. Brown would answer, but it kept ringing until I picked it up. I knew before I heard her voice that it was Susan. "Ronnie, I need your help."

"I'm trying to help you, Susan. What do you want me to do."

"Go to my apartment, look in the closet in my bedroom, you'll find a briefcase there, bring it back here, and you will find what you need to help me."

"It may not be there because the police have been all over your apartment; they probably found the briefcase already."

"No, they haven't. No one knows about the briefcase, so they wouldn't know where to look to find it."

I'll go tomorrow and get it. Susan, can you tell me what this is all about? And how is it that I can talk to you and see you, and no one else can?"

"I don't know; maybe it's because we were so close in life, and you were the only one who understood me."

"Susan, what going on? What happens to you? Do you know who kill you and why?"

"Ronnie, remember the guy I told you I was seeing? I'm pretty sure he was involved with my death. You see, I did some work for him on the side, and it turned out to be more than I was bargaining for. I thought I could handle it, but I guess I was wrong. I didn't know I was in so deep until I read some papers he gave me on my own. So I went to him about what I found and asked him to explain what was going on. He told me to mind my own business. That it was not my concern and to do what I was told and no more.

So I did for a while, and the more I found out, the more I wanted out. I didn't want to work for him anymore. But he wouldn't let me out. I told him I was going to the police and that when things got bad. I guess threatening him with the law was a bad idea. I didn't know how powerful he was. He told me I wouldn't do that if I were you, that bad thing could happen to nice people, and he didn't want to see anything happen to me.

I should've listened to him, but I wanted out so bad. I told him if I had known that this was the kind of work I was doing for him, I would stop a long time ago. Money laundering. Drugs, offshore bank accounts. I didn't know why my boss would do this to me. To hook me up with someone like him, I still don't understand the reason."

"I do because you're blond, and they believe what people said about blond. But that was not true about you. You were smart and beautiful."

"That's why I need your help. Please, Ronnie, you the only one who can do this for me."

"Of course, I will help you, Susan; after all, you were my blue eyes friend."

"I love you, Ronnie."

"I love you, Susan. I'll do what I can, but I'm a little afraid. What if I get caught looking around? What if your friend has someone watching your apartment?"

"Don't worry. I won't let anything happen to you. I'll let you know when it's safe to go to the apartment."

"I wish you were here so we could do this together." I will be. The only thing is you are the only one who will know or see me."

"Okay, I'll get started tomorrow."

Then the phone went dead; I don't mean she hung up, no, the phone just went dead, no dial tone or anything.

I hung up the phone and just sat there, wondering what I should do. When the phone rang again, I thought it was Susan, "Susan?" I said.

"No, not Susan Office Jackson. Why did you answer the phone like that? Were you expecting to hear your friend on the other end of the phone?"

"Not really. I was sitting here thinking of Susan that all."

"Why are you calling?"

"I'm calling to see if you wanted to have dinner with me tonight?"

"Tonight? I don't know. I thought I would give you a break this evening."

"Why? You don't want to have dinner with me?"

"No, it's not that it's just that you have taken me out for the past three days, and I thought you would be tired of me by now."

"No, never. Jean told me you were by the restaurant today with a friend."

"No, she was not a friend, just a co-worker of Susan."

"How did you meet her?"

"She called and asked me out to lunch."

"You didn't know her before today?"

"Never met or heard of her until today."

"What did she want?"

"I don't know exactly; mostly, she asked about what Susan was like when she was young and growing up in Chicago."

"That's it? Nothing else, nothing about the job your friend was working on?"

"No, I don't think she talked about anything like that."

"Are you sure?"

"Yes, I'm sure. Why are you asking me all these questions? I thought you were calling to ask me out tonight?"

"I was. I just wanted to know about your friend coworker."

"About tonight, I don't think I will go out with you. I believe I'll stay in."

"Okay, if you sure, then I'll talk to you in the morning, have a good night."

"Thank you, good night."

CHAPTER NINETEEN

I couldn't sleep. All I could do was think about what I had heard on the phone before Office Jackson had called. I wondered if it was Susan I was speaking to, or was it my imagination? But I knew Susan's voice. I knew just how it sounded. We were together all the time when we were kids, so I knew her voice when I heard it. I stayed in the room until about ten o'clock then I went into the living room. Mrs. Brown and her sister must have gone out to dinner because I was alone. So I called room service and ordered myself a sandwich. While I waited for it to be brought up, I thought about what Susan and I had talked about on the phone. I loved Susan and wanted to find out who killed her, but I was also afraid. I thought that maybe I should talk to Office Jackson, but I knew he would think I was crazy.

The next day I called the police station to speak to Officer Jackson. He hadn't made it into work yet. I asked if they could have him call me when he got in. "What is this concerning?" They wanted to know.

"Would it be ok to go over to my friend Susan's apartment today and get some of her things packed up?

I don't see why not; I think they are through going over the crime scene. I'll have Officer Jackson give you a call when he gets in.

I went over to the apartment before I talked to Officer Jackson. I didn't tell. Mrs. Brown, I was going over there she might have asked to come with me, and I wanted to do this alone. It felt strange to be in Susan's apartment. It looked like someone had tried to clean it up at first glance, but when I opened the bedroom door, I could see that wasn't the case. I stood there looking and wondering who could have killed my beautiful blue-eyed friend. I shut the door to the bedroom and sat down on a chair in the living room. I don't know how long I sat there before realizing I wasn't alone anymore.

I looked up, and there sitting across from me, was my friend the way she was when we graduated from college.

"Hi," I said. How long have you been sitting there?

"Not long. I've been looking around the apartment for the last time. You know I loved this place. I always wanted you to see it, but not like this. I thought that you would come, and we would do New York only the way we could."

"I wish I had come too. I'm sorry I didn't."

"It wasn't your fault things change; we changed. We had our own lives to live."

"Yes, but that is no reason for us to have lost touch the way we did."

"I know. Oh, Ronnie, I'm sorry I wish things could have been different. I wish you would've come to New York when we first got out of college; it would have been so much fun."

"I know, but you knew how my parents were. I accept it, they were my parents, and I love them very much."

"I know," Susan said.

"Susan, why are you here?"

"I want you to tell the police who killed me and why."

"How am I going to accomplish that? I don't know the people you knew, and I don't know the places you would go."

"I'll help you. In my bedroom, there is a panel in the back of the closet; no one knows it's there. They wouldn't know where to look even if they did. No one did, not even John. In the closet, there's a switch. Push it in the back under the end of the carpet, and the wall will open. In there, you will find some paper, and some print out gets them out and take them to the police. But before you do, make some copies of them and keep them somewhere safe. You might need them again."

"Why would I need them? I don't know anything about your business."

"Trust me, make a copy, and keep them safe."

I got up, went into the bedroom, and did what Susan told me. The papers were there, and the printouts were also just like Susan said.

I took them, wondering what they were and how could I help Susan with them? I found a briefcase in the closet and put the papers in it. I turned to leave the closet, stopped, and looked again at the bed. I started to cry. I don't know why I just couldn't stop the tears from coming. It was true. It was really, really true. I was never going to see my friend again.

Susan, the girl with beautiful blue eyes and long blond hair, I would never see her again. The only person I could laugh with, cry with, the one person I could count on if I really needed her help. I stood there, remembering all the things we had gone through when we were kids. How we became instant friends and how she used to stand up for me when she thought I wouldn't do it for myself or if I wasn't fast enough in doing so. How we used to go to the mall and if we saw something we both liked, we didn't mind getting the same things and wearing them on the same day.

We didn't care what people thought of us; we were friends, which was enough for us. I cried because I would miss her laugh and the way her eyes would sparkle when she got into mischief or how she would call me in the middle of the night when our parents were asleep. I'm was going to miss my blue eyes friend truly.

I turned to walk out of the room, but I couldn't stop looking at the bed for some reason. So I walked over to it. I didn't want to touch it, but I couldn't help myself for some reason. I didn't know what I was looking for or what I was supposed to see if anything. So I just stood there, stirring at the bed. Something wasn't right. I knew I hadn't been in here before, but I knew something wasn't right with the bed.

I touch the headboard. I didn't know what was going on or what I might find; all I knew was there was something there. I felt the headboard and the covers, and I stood back and looked at the bed; then it came to me what I was looking at, and I stepped back again. I couldn't believe what I had just seen. (Oh my god,

I saw how Susan died, and I know who killed her and how they did it.) I left the bedroom and went back into the living room; I turned around to say something to Susan, but she wasn't there, I called out to her, but she didn't answer. So I took the briefcase and left the apartment.

CHAPTER TWENTY

I went back to the hotel, where Mrs. Brown and her sister were about to go out for lunch.

"Hello, Veronica. Where have you been this morning?" Mrs. Brown asked.

"I went for a walk together, my thoughts. I didn't want to disturb you."

"You were gone for a long time. Have you had lunch yet?" she asked.

"No, not yet."

"Would you like to go with Melissa and me?"

"No, that's alright, you two go ahead. I think I'll just stay here for a while."

"You're sure?"

"Yes," I told her.

"Come on, Gloria, she said that she didn't want to go."

"Melissa, I told you to stop giving Veronica a hard time. I meant it."

They left. I sat there thinking about what I found at Susan's apartment. I wondered if I should call CJ and let him know what I had found, and just when I thought I had made up my mind, I looked up and saw Susan standing in the corner.

"What are you doing here?"

"I don't think you should tell your friend right now about what you found," she said.

"Why not? Don't you think he'll believe me?"

"That not the point."

"What is the point?"

"The point is your friend will want to know where you got the information. So what are you going to tell him? Oh, my friend came to me and told me where to look. So what do you think he'll say to that?"

"I don't think he'll say anything, but he will wonder. Okay, what do you want me to do?"

"You'll know when the time is right."

"When the time is right? Susan, we will be going home soon."

"Why didn't you go to lunch with my mother?" she said, changing the subject.

"I wasn't hungry, and besides, your aunt was with her, and you know we don't get along."

"Susan, how can we be talking like this? I mean, you're gone."

"Not gone dead."

"What?"

"I'm not gone; I'm dead."

"I know."

"Then why do you say gone instead of dead?"

"Because if I say dead, I'll never see you again. So I say gone, so then I know I might see you again someday."

"Oh, Ronnie, I'm going to miss you the most of everything in this world."

"I'm going to miss you too. You were the only person I really could talk to about anything."

"Susan? What am I supposed to do with this information?"

"Hold on to it until the end of the day, and then I will tell you what to do with it." Ronnie, promise me that———-someone is coming."

"Promise you what? Susan, promise you what? Susan? Susan?"

CHAPTER TWENTY-ONE

"Miss Smith? Veronica? A knocking on the door brought me back from talking to Susan.

"Coming, yes, who is it?"

"It's me, Office Jackson. "I was coming by to talk to you when I heard you call out. Are you alright?"

"Yes, just a minute." I opened the door, and there he was, standing there looking as if he wanted to save me from a monster or something. I just stood there looking at him.

"Are you sure you alright?"

"Yes, I'm."

"Are you sure?"

"I must've felt off to sleep and had a dream that all."

"Would you like to tell me about it?" he asked.

"No. what are you doing here?"

"I stopped by to tell you and Mrs. Brown that things are about wrapped up, and you should be able to leave by Saturday. Is she here?"

"Is who here?"

"Mrs. Brown, is she here?"

"No, she went out to lunch with her sister. I'll let her know you stopped by."

"Veronica, would you go out with me tonight? I mean to dinner and maybe a show?"

"I can't."

"Why not?"

"I don't have anything to wear, and I need to go to the beauty shop because my hair is a mess."

"That's okay, I could ask Jean to take you shopping, and as for your hair, it looks just beautiful to me."

"I couldn't ask your sister to take off from her job to help me find a dress to go out with you. And my hair doesn't look beautiful; it's a mess. So therefore, I cannot go out with you tonight. But, I will tell Gloria that you came by."

He stood there looking at me for a few seconds, smiled, then turned and left.

About an hour later, I got a call from his sister Jean.

CHAPTER-TWENTY-TWO

"Hello Ronnie, I'm downstairs in the lobby and was wondering, would you like to go shopping with me? It's been months since I had a day off, so I decided to take one today and do a little shopping and wanted you to go with me if you're not busy?"

"Did your brother put you up to this?" I asked her.

"My brother? Whatever gave you that idea?"

"Because he was here about an hour ago and asked if I would like to go out to a movie and dinner, and I told him I didn't have anything to wear."

"Well, okay, you got me, he did ask me to take you shopping, and I did jump at the idea because it been so long since I had a reason to go or had a day off. Please, Ronnie, go with me, you don't have to buy a thing if you don't want to. And I know the perfect place you can go to get your hair fix if you want to, that is."

"Okay, I'll be right down." I stopped and looked around for Susan, but I didn't see her, so I went to the lobby to meet Jean.

"So, how have you been?"

"Fine, Jean, I want you to know that's it's a probability I won't go out with your brother tonight."

"Why? Don't you like my brother?"

"Yes, I like him, but I just want to get this stuff with Susan finished so I can go home. I don't want things to get serious between your brother and me, not saying that it will. I just don't want to get hurt."

"And you think that CJ would hurt you?"

"Yes."

"Why?" she asked.

"Jean, I never had a boyfriend before, and I don't want to get hurt. Will this one boy I liked, and I thought he liked me, he even asked me to the senior prom? I was so happy that he asked. I told my parents. They were so pleased that he had asked me. They thought he was a nice boy, but it turned out to be a joke. I told you about how Susan and I could hear other people's thoughts sometimes; will I was walking by his locker one day about a week before the prom, and I heard his thoughts about how silly and hurt I would be when he didn't show up on prom night."

"He didn't?"

"Yes, he did. I asked him about it. He asked me who had told me about it. I told him I heard it around and that I wasn't going to prom with him so that I wouldn't be waiting for him on prom night.

"Ronnie, I'm so sorry he did that to you. What did your parents say?"

"Nothing, I never told them. I pertained I was sick that day, so I wouldn't have to explain. After that, I stay away from boys. Don't get me wrong; I would've liked to have had a boyfriend. I just don't want to be made fun of."

"My brother wouldn't make fun of you; he likes you."

"How could he? He just met me. He doesn't know anything about me. How could he? Just look at me. I'm not pretty like most girls, and I'm too short, and my hair—- well, just look at me who in their right mind would want to be with me?"

"You shouldn't feel that way about yourself."

"I don't. It's just what I heard people say about me—— everyone but Susan. I could talk to her about anything, about the way people treated me. Susan understood even when I was a child, she understood.

My parents knew that why they tried to keep me away from people. But I knew, and Susan knew too, but she was my friend, the only one I had. But now—- (I started to cry). I'm sorry, Jean. I can't go shopping with you. I'm sorry."

"That okay; maybe I can call you later to see if you're alright?"

"If you want to? Tell your brother that I'm sorry about tonight. I just can't go out with him." So I went back upstairs and did something I hadn't done in a long time—- cry myself to sleep.

CHAPTER-TWENTY-THREE

I didn't know what time it was when I woke up. It could have been fifteen-minute or two hours. I didn't know how long I'd been sleeping. The ringing of the phone woke me up. Hello?

"Ms. Smith, this is the front desk. There's a gentleman down here who would like to speak to you. Is it alright to send him up?"

"I don't know; who is he?"

"Just a second, I'll ask."

I heard him asking the man his name. I never heard it before.

"He said his name is Justin Wheeler."

"I don't know any Justin Wheeler."

"He claims to have known your friend Susan Brown."

"Susan never mentions him to me. Tell him I'll be right down, or better still, tell him I'll be down in five minutes."

I stood there wondering who this man was and how did he know I was Susan's friend? Finally, I washed my face and went down. I forgot to ask what the man looked like, but it was no need, for as soon as I stepped off the elevator, a very handsome man walked up to me. Ms. Smith?

"Yes?"

"I'm Justin Wheeler, a friend of Susan."

"Yes, I know," I said.

"You know? Susan much had mentioned me then."

"No, she didn't. I never heard of you until the man at the desk called up and said you wanted to see me."

"Well, how did you know who I was?" he asked.

"Is there something I can do for you, Mr. Wheeler?"

"Yes, first, let me say that I'm sorry for your lost."

"Thank you, and second?"

"What?"

"You said first, so I figure it had to be a second."

"Well, not a second. I was just wondering did you happen to find a briefcase in Susan's apartment."

"No, should I have?"

"I just thought that maybe you had."

"Why would you think that?"

"Because you been to her apartment."

"Yes, but the police have been there too. Why don't you ask them about this briefcase?"

"I just figure you had it or had seen it."

"No, I haven't. What in it? Is it anything important?'

"No, not really. If you do see it, could you give me a call?"

"It's possible I won't. You see, I'll be leaving in a few days and don't see a need to go back to Susan's apartment again."

"Well, just in case you do happen to go and find it could you give me a call?"

"Alright, I will, Mr. Wheeler." I turned to leave when he touched my arm.

"Would you like to have dinner with me tonight?" he asked.

I stare at him. He was a nice-looking man, and I wonder why he would want to have dinner with me? "No, thank you. I said politely."

"Why? he wanted to know.

I looked up and saw Susan's mother coming in. "I'm having dinner with friends."

"Hello, Veronica. Did you have a pleasant day? Gloria asked.

"Yes, it was okay. Gloria, I would like you to meet Mr. Justin Wheeler, a friend of Susan."

"Mr. Wheeler, how are you? I'm Susan's mother, and this is her Aunt Melissa."

"Ladies, he said.

Turning back to me, he said, "If you change your mind, you can give me a call at the number on the card." He turned and left.

"Who was that?"

"Claims to be a friend of Susan."

"What did he want? Melissa wanted to know.

"Said he was looking for a briefcase he left at Susan's apartment," I said.

"What did you tell him?" Melissa asked.

"That I didn't know what he was talking about. That I hadn't found anything at Susan's apartment."

"Will did you?" Susan's aunt asked.

"Did I what?"

"Find anything at Susan's apartment?"

"No, I didn't. I didn't come here to go through her things to see what she had.

Gloria, Officer Jackson came by saying that they should be finished with everything by the end of the week." I told her as we stepped out of the elevator.

"That will be fine, then maybe we will be able to start putting this behind us," She said.

"Will we have the funeral here or back home?"

"I thought about having it back home. Then I figured I would have it here since this is where she been living for the past seven years."

"Would you like me to get in touch with a funeral home for you?" I could ask Officer Jackson to recommend one if you like.

"Yes, why don't you do that?"

"I'll give him a call in the morning," I told her.

CHAPTER TWENTY-FOUR

The following day I got up at about seven o'clock. I didn't know what time Officer Jackson went to work, so I called the station to talk to him.

"May I speak to Officer Jackson?"

He doesn't start until eight o'clock. Who calling?

Veronica Smith. I spoke to him yesterday. I just needed his help with something. I'll give him a callback.

I didn't get around to calling Officer Jackson. I had been out with Susan's mother trying to find a nice funeral home on our own. Then we tried to get in touch with all of Susan's relatives to let them know that the funeral would be in New York the following week. Gloria said that it would be on Wednesday. So I was busy helping out. So I forgot to call. I was just getting up to go to lunch when the phone rang. It was Officer Jackson.

"Hello Veronica, you called looking for me this morning?"

"Oh, yes, I forgot."

"What did you want?" he asked.

"I was calling for Mrs. Brown, Gloria. She wanted to know if you knew of any funeral home in this area that was not too expensive?"

"I don't know. I haven't had any use for one since my parents died, and that was a long time ago."

"You didn't let me finish you weren't in, so we look for one on our own; I think we found a very affordable one. The services will be next Wednesday if that okay?"

"That should be all right. Are you leaving right after the services?"

"No, Gloria asked me if I would take care of Susan's things for her after the services because she has to return home the day after."

"Good, I'll get a chance to see you then."

"I guess so. Officer Jackson, I'm sorry about last night. I still can't understand why you want to see me?"

"Have you eaten?" he asked.

"No, not yet. I was on my way when you called."

"Have lunch with me, and I'll tell you the reason why."

"Okay, I'll have to change. Give me about twenty minutes?"

"Twenty minutes it is. I'll be waiting in the lobby. Is that alright?

"No, can you come up?" I asked.

"I'll be there in twenty minutes, if not sooner."

Okay, twenty minutes, Veronica said.

I don't know what made me say that I'll have lunch with him and I was looking forward to it. So I went into the bedroom to change, and there on the end of the bed, sat Susan. "I'm glad you are having lunch with CJ," she said.

"Me too. How did you know I called him that?"

"That doesn't matter right now. I need to talk to you.

We can talk while you change," Susan said.

"Okay, what's up?" It felt good talking to Susan; it felt like old times when we were getting ready to go out somewhere together.

"Remember the briefcase you got out of my apartment?" I need you to give it to CJ.

"Why."

"Because it had some very important papers in it, and I don't want Justin to get his hands on it."

"Is Justin the man you were involved with?"

"No, he is a friend of John. He isn't a very nice person. He does whatever John asks him to do. I need you to give the case to Officer Jackson right away before you meet with Justin again."

"Meet with Justin again? I have no plans to meet with him again. I told him I didn't know anything about what was going on with you."

"He doesn't believe you. You look stunning in that dress, Ronnie."

"Do you like it?"

"Yes, it's very nice, and I like your hair down like that. Officer Jackson is going to fall head over heels for you."

"I am not trying to impress Officer Jackson; besides, why would he want someone like me anyway?"

"Ronnie, you still don't know how beautiful you are?"

"I'm not beautiful. I'm just not bad to look at."

"Your parents really did a number on you. But, Ronnie, you are beautiful and kind and funny, and all those things you just have to believe it and don't let anyone tell you yours not."

"I have to go. Will you be here when I get back?"

"I don't know, Ronnie. Please be careful and remember what I told you about Justin."

"I'll be careful, don't worry."

CHAPTER TWENTY-FIVE

I left and forgot all about what Susan and I had talked about. I don't know why it just slipped my mind completely. I came out of the bedroom, and CJ was waiting for me. I don't know why I was so excited to see him. I thought you can't let him see your excitement, or he might not want to see you anymore.

"Are you ready?" he asked.

"Mrs. Brown said she would see you for dinner," he told me.

As we got off the elevator, heads turned to look my way, but I didn't notice. All I could see was Officer Jackson in front of me.

"Do you have any idea how beautiful you are? he asked me.

I lower my head. I didn't want him to see me blush.

"So were, are we going for lunch?"

"Anywhere everywhere, I got the day off, so we can do whatever you want."

"I've never been to New York before, so you can decide where to go to lunch."

I hadn't noticed that he wasn't in his uniform. He has dressed in a nice pair of navy blue slacks and a light blue shirt. He looked very nice in them.

"Would you like to go to my sister's restaurant for lunch?"

"Yes, that would be alright. I should apologize for not going shopping with her yesterday."

We walk down central park over to fifth to the restaurant. When we got there, it was crowded. Jean was at a table, talking to some customers. She turned and saw us by the door.

"Well, look who's here. You looking stunning today, Ronnie, and your hair, I like it like that."

"Thank you; I'm sorry about yesterday; I just had so much on my mind."

"That's okay. You're here now and with my brother, no less. So, brother, I see you're out of uniform. Does this mean you got the day off?"

"Yes, I do and thought I bring Veronica by for lunch. So do you mind showing us to a table?" he joked with his sister.

"I got just the one follow me." She led us to one right in front by the window.

"I don't know. This is too close to the window, don't you think?" Veronica asked.

"No, I don't. I think this is just the right place to show you off," CJ said.

"But I don't want to be shown off. I dress this way for you and you alone."

"That was very kind of you, but don't you think this is an excellent table? No one will bother us here, and we can talk."

"Okay, if this is where you want to sit, then I guess it's okay," I told him.

CHAPTER TWENTY-SIX

I had the most wonderful time I ever had in my life. I forgot all about Susan and the briefcase she wants me to give CJ.

"So, you will be leaving soon," CJ said.

"Yes, in about a week, Gloria asked if I would close up Susan's apartment for her. I told her that I would. I told her she should take anything she wanted out of there before leaving. She said all she wanted was some pictures of Susan she had seen while there. Will you be coming to the services?"

"Would you like me to?" he asked with a smile.

"Yes, I don't mean to put you on the spot by asking. It's just that I would like for you to be there if you can."

"I'll see what my schedule looks like and get back to you, okay?"

Just then, Jean walked up. "Have you decided on what you wanted?" she asked.

I look up at her with a smile. I'll let CJ order for me because a burger would do just fine by me."

"You want a burger?" she asked, surprise

"No, not here. We don't have to eat a burger here; we could have gone to a fast food place for a burger. Let CJ order for us, please."

"She looked at CJ and smiled; so what do you want on your burger today?" She asked him.

"We'll have two burgers with the works. How would you like yours cooked, Veronica?"

"I guess I'll have it the way he has his if that okay?"

"Fine, two medium burgers with everything coming right up," she said and left.

"You didn't have to do that. We could eat something else."

"No, you don't understand. I love Jean burgers; they have a taste all their own, and you haven't tasted anything until you tasted one of her burgers, trust me."

"If you say so. But we could eat something else if you had wanted," I said.

I turned and looked out the window, and there standing across the street, was this man just staring at me.

"That's strange?" I wonder aloud.

"What?" CJ asked

"That man, he seems to be staring at me."

"Do you know him?" he asked.

"I don't know anyone here in New York, so why would he be looking at me?"

"Maybe he is just looking this way," CJ said.

"No, I think he's staring at me."

"No, I don't believe so; see, he's walking away now. Maybe he was looking for someone who didn't show up."

"Maybe you're right," I said. Still not too sure I believe that.

"So what would you like to do after lunch?" he asked me with a smile.

(He had the most beautiful smile I ever seen on anyone.) "I don't know whatever you want; we could go for a walk if that okay? I said.

"That's fine. Where would you like to walk?"

"You decide. You know better than I do."

"Well, let's just walk and see where it takes us."

Just then, Jean came back with our lunch. "Here you go. I hope they're okay."

(we eat in silence)

She came back a little while later. "Are the burger okay?"

"Yes, they're fine, the best burger I ever tasted. They tasted great." I told her.

"I told you, Jean makes the best burger in the city," CJ said

"So, the funeral is Wednesday?" Jean asked

"Yes, Gloria is waiting for some family member to get into town," I told her.

"Do you think they will come?"

"I don't know it's possible. Everyone loved Susan. Gloria will be leaving the next day, but she asked me to stay and close Susan, apartment for her. So I'll be leaving Friday."

"Can you stay longer?" Jean asked

"I wish I could, but I can't. I have my own business to run. It may not be much, but it's all I got. I've been gone long enough."

"Do you think you will come back to New York anytime soon?" Officer Jackson asked.

"No, I don't think, so there isn't any reason for me to come back."

"You don't think so? Not even for me?"

"I don't know—- maybe." I turned and looked out the window, and the same man was looking in my direction. I didn't think anything of it; he looked this way but not at me. I didn't tell CJ about it. I thought that maybe he would think I was being paranoid. We finished lunch and went for our walking. It was the best time I ever had. I didn't want to tell him that. I didn't want him to know that I like him maybe a little. Okay, a lot.

CHAPTER TWENTY-SEVEN

We walked for about an hour or so, and then he took me back to the hotel. Gloria and her sister were just coming in.

"How was your day, dear?" Gloria asked.

Fine, I had a very nice time with Officer Jackson. We went out to lunch and for a walk."

"How are you doing, Office Jackson?" She asked.

"Fine, Veronica was telling me that you're thinking about having the funeral on Wednesday?"

"Yes, I am. I need to get back home, and Susan has been out here since she got out of college. So I figure this is the place she would want to be laid to rest."

"I think maybe you're right. Hopefully, we will have some more information for you by then. Goodbye, maybe I will see you later?"

"I don't know, perhaps tomorrow. Thank you for a lovely afternoon."

"It was my pleasure; he smiled." And he turned and walked away.

"I do like that, Officer Jackson," Mrs. Brown said, looking at me with a smile. I smiled and got on the elevator.

Once in the suite, I went to my room, and Susan was sitting there on the bed. "You didn't tell him about Justin, did you?" She asked.

"Oh no, Susan, I forgot. I'm sorry I had such a good time. I forgot."

"You need to tell him right away, Ronnie," she said.

"I will, I promise."

"But you only got two more days. Oh, Ronnie, I don't want anything to happen to you. You much tell him right away. You don't know John like I do."

"I'll tell him tomorrow. I don't think I'll be seeing him again before then."

"Alright, tomorrow, don't forget and give him the briefcase too that the importance piece he will need."

The following day we went to view the body. Susan looked so peaceful lying there; she looked like she was sleeping. We had made all the arrangements, so there was nothing else to do but wait until Wednesday for the services. So I went back to the hotel. But I just couldn't get comfortable for some reason. I tried to read, and that didn't do any good. So I went back to my bedroom, and Susan was sitting on the bed.

"Susan, I'm so glad to see you."

"Why haven't you given CJ the briefcase yet?"

"I'm waiting for him to call; he wasn't at work when I phoned this morning, so I left a message for him to get in touch with me."

"Okay, that's good. Maybe he'll call this afternoon."

"You know, Susan, Wednesday is your services. Will I see you anymore after then?"

"I don't know. I don't understand why you can see me now, but I'm glad that you can."

"Me too. You were the only real friend I ever had. You were like the sister I never had. You were the only person who never made fun of me. I try to fit in, but for some reason, I never could. But that didn't seem to matter to you."

"Why should it? We got along beautifully together. You like what I like, and I like what you like, so why not? Veronica, you were the sister I never had."

My parents never wanted any more children, so I thought that I would be alone all my life than you came along. I was so happy to see you on that first day. I knew something was different about you when I thought I heard you talking to me. But you weren't. I heard you in my mind. You were saying, don't worry; it will be alright, I won't let anyone mess with you. Then you can up to me and said: "Hi, my name is Susan Brown." You didn't even ask me my name. "You just said come on, Ronnie, everything will be alright" and took my hand, and everything was alright.

"I don't know if I ever told you this, Susan, but I love you then, and I love you now. I have always loved you."

"And I have always loved you, Veronica. You will never know how much. You were the only person I could depend on. You were always there for me. I remember when I would call you about some boy or another, you would just listen to what I had to say. And then try to make me feel better by telling me he wasn't good enough for me and that I deserved better than that for myself. If it wasn't for you, no telling what would happen with my life."

"Maybe if I hadn't left you alone, you wouldn't be dead now," I told her.

"You are not to blame for what happened to me, Veronica. If you had been here, you would have been able to stop me from making some of the mistakes I did, but not all of them."

"Why do you keep calling me Veronica and not Ronnie? I don't think I ever heard you call me anything but Ronnie all my life unless there was something you wanted me to do or I wasn't paying attention to what you were saying to me, and now you keep calling me Veronica; why?"

"I didn't want to tell you this, but I'm going to have to leave you. I don't know if it will be forever, but I will be leaving you."

"When? Why?"

"I don't know; it could be today or tomorrow or the next minute, I don't know. I just know that I'll be leaving soon."

"No, Susan, you can't go. Please don't leave me alone again.; things haven't been the same since you left. I don't have any friends. No one will talk to me like you did. I don't have a boyfriend; in fact, I never had one. So please don't leave me."

"But you told me you did."

"I know I just didn't want you to feel sorry for me. I never had a boyfriend, I never been kissed, isn't that funny?" I started to cry.

"But why, Ronnie? You are so beautiful you could have had any guys you wanted when we were in school. And I thought you did."

"Remember, Susan, when people used to call me your little *nigger* friend?"

"No, I don't remember that."

"That right, I forgot that sometimes I could hear people's thoughts, and you couldn't."

"But you never said anything to me about it."

"I thought, why should I tell you? You had your life to live, and you couldn't come to my rescue all the time someone said something about me, so I just smiled when you were around and took it."

"I wish you would have told me. I'm sorry you were so unhappy."

"That just it. I wasn't unhappy when you were around because we could do things no one else could do. We could talk, and no one could hear us even if we were in a different room. We could still talk to one another. Remember that class we were in at different hours? I don't remember exactly what class it was now, but remember we had a test and you hadn't studied for it and I was in my English class and I heard you say "I wish Ronnie were here to help me with this." Remember I said, "I'm here; what do you need?"

"Yes, I remember you gave me all the answers. I got A on that test. But that still doesn't tell me why you didn't tell me what was going on."

"Because we were in high school and some things I needed to handle myself, and besides, I thought you could hear them too and just didn't care. So I figure why should I. Why let it bother me when it didn't bother you."

"I wish you would have told me."

"I almost did."

"When?" Remember one day we were at lunch, and I asked you could you hear what Valerie was saying, and you said no."

"You asked me to tell you, and I said, never mind."

"Yes, I remember that."

"That, when I learned that I could hear what you couldn't from other people."

Just then, the phone rang. "I'll be right back."

"That was Officer Jackson. He said he'd come over on his lunch break."

"Good, then you can tell him what I told you and give him the briefcase."

"No, we can tell him together if you're here. I don't want to make any mistakes."

"Alright, I'll try to be here when he comes. I love you, Veronica Marie Smith, more than anyone in this world, and don't you ever forget it now go take your shower."

"How did you know I wanted to take a shower? Never mind, I forgot we can still read each other minds even now."

CHAPTER TWENTY-EIGHT

I was just getting out of the shower when there was a knock on the door. "Just a minute," I said. I went to the door and turned the knob to open it, thinking that it was Officer Jackson when Susan appeared and shouted, "Don't open it," but it was too late the door opened and there stood the man who had been following me all of yesterday. I couldn't move. I just stood there staring at him, wondering what to do.

"Who are you, and what are you doing in my hotel room?" I asked him.

"You know who I am. I'm a friend of John and Susan, and I come for some information I know you have."

"Information? What information? What are you talking about, and who are you?" I could hear Susan whispering, "Be careful, Ronnie. I don't know who this man is"

"I know."

"You know what?" he asked.

You're the man I saw yesterday. "What do you want?" I asked him instead.

"The briefcase."

"What briefcase?"

"The one you took from Ms. Brown's apartment the other day."

"I didn't take any briefcase from Susan's apartment, and if I did so, what?"

"Mr. Wheeler would like to have it back."

"Is it Mr. Wheeler?"

"No."

"Then why would he want something that doesn't belong to him?"

"Just give me the case, lady."

"I don't have anything to give you. Would you please leave?"

"Not till I get what I can for."

"I told you I don't have anything." Be careful, Ronnie; you don't know what Justin told him to do to get that case.

"I know."

"You know what?" he asked again.

"Nothing. I want to get dressed now if you don't mind." I was still standing in my robe. Just then, the phone ringed. I just stood there.

"Aren't you going to get that?" he asked.

"Yes. And I also would like to get dressed, please."

I moved toward the phone. I heard Susan say; it's just the front desk calling to see if everything is alright. I made the doorman call up; when you answer, just say yes, then act like it is CJ you're talking to and be sure you call him by name, trust me.

I picked up the phone, and it was the front desk, just like Susan said, checking to make sure everything was okay.

"Fine," I said.

Okay, he said, "are you sure?"

"Yes," I said, and he hung up.

I kept talking like I was talking to Officer Jackson. "Officer Jackson, I'll be right down. I'm just getting dressed. Would you like to come up? Will I guess that will be alright? I'll leave the door open for you. I'll see you in a bit? Okay bye.

I turned around, and the man was gone. I let out a breath of relief. "Thanks, Susan. How did you know to do that?" I asked her.

"It just came to me. I'm not the only one watching over you."

"Now listen, you go get dressed, and then go find CJ and tell him what I told you."

"But what if he's at work?"

"Then you stay there until he gets off. I don't want you to be by yourself for the rest of the day, understand?"

"Yes."

CHAPTER TWENTY-NINE

I dressed and went down to the police station where Officer Jackson worked. He had just gone out on a call, and they didn't know how long it was going to take. If I would like to leave my name and where he could get in touch with me, they would give him the message.

I started to leave a message when I heard Susan saying, "just sit over there and wait."

I turned back and said, "I'll just wait over there if it's alright?"

"Suit yourself, lady; it may be a while."

"That okay. I'll wait." I sat there for what seemed like hours, and then Office Jackson came in. I never was so happy to see anyone in my whole life. Not just because he could help me with Susan, but with him, I felt safe, and I haven't felt this safe since I was a child living with my parents.

"Jackson, someone waiting to see you. She's been here for hours." She's quite a looker. He turned to see who it was and when he saw that it was me his face just lit up.

"What are you doing here?" he asked.

"I hope you don't mind me coming here, but I had to talk to you right away."

"No, I don't mind. What is it?"

"It's about Susan."

"What about Susan? What's wrong you're shaking like a leaf?"

"A man came to see today...."

"What, man? Who was he?"

"I don't know. He was the man we saw across the street at lunch yesterday.

"What did he want?"

"That's what I'm trying to tell you; he wants a briefcase of Susan that I have."

"What briefcase? Where did you get it from?" he wanted to know.

"I got it from her apartment," I told him.

"We looked all over that apartment didn't find any briefcase."

"I know Susan had hidden it. She told me where to find it."

"Was this before you came to New York?"

"No, since I have been here."

"Why didn't you tell me about the briefcase before now?"

"I—-I forgot about it."

"You forgot? how could you forget something so important?"

"I don't know. All I know is the guy you're looking for is Justin wheeler.

"Who is this person?"

"He's the man who came to see me the other day. He was asking me about the briefcase. I didn't know what he was talking about than not until Susan told me about it later. He had this man following me for days."

"Why didn't you tell me this sooner?" he asked.

"I don't know. I meant to tell you at lunch, but I was so happy to see you, I forgot."

"You were glad to see me?" he said with a smile.

"Yes, but that's beside the point right now. That man is after the briefcase Susan told me to get. Susan told me to give it to you. Will you come with me now and get it?"

Just then, a call came in that he had to go on. I can't now, but I'll be by later to get the case from you. So just sit tight, and I'll be over to pick it up later.

"Okay, I'll be waiting for you at the hotel."

CHAPTER THIRTY

I went back to the hotel, and Mrs. Brown and her sister were there.
"How are you, Ronnie?" Mrs. Brown asked.
"I fine, just a little tired."
"We just came from making the final arrangements for Susan's services tomorrow. The service will be at three o'clock in the afternoon."
"That soon? I thought they were to be on Wednesday?"
"Yes, the police called and said we could have Susan later today, and I wanted to put her in the ground as soon as possible. She's been out too long as it is."
"Yes, I understand it has been a while."
"Yes, I thought that I could go back home the day after tomorrow. What wrong, dear?"
"Nothing. I thought that you were going to have her flown back to Chicago?" I said absentmindedly. I was still thinking about what had happened earlier.
"I was then I thought this is where she was living, so maybe she wanted to be laid to rest here too. I decide to do it here.
"I'm going to miss her so much. I know it's been years since I saw her, but I'll miss her just the same."
I started to cry. Mrs. Brown came over and took me in her arms. "There, there, dear, I'll miss Susan too. I'm glad she had a friend like you. I never could understand the relationship you two had, but I'm

happy that you were friends. Someone she could share her thoughts with. I thought you would like to help me pick out her last outfit."

"I would like that, but shouldn't you let your sister help you? She was Susan's aunt."

"No, you were her best friend. Besides, Susan never did get along with her aunt."

"Well then, I know just the outfit. I saw it the other day when I was at the apartment."

"What were you doing at Susan's apartment?" her mother asked.

"She asked me to go and pick something up for her."

"Who told you to do what?"

I stopped and looked around. Susan was standing there, smiling. She knew I had said too much.

"I meant to say I saw it when we went there the other day."

"Are you sure that what you meant?" Susan's aunt asked.

"Yes. When do you want me to get it? I could go now if you want?"

"That will be all right."

(I had forgotten all about the man outside the building who had been following me.) I went into the bedroom, Susan was there.

"Be careful, Ronnie, please be careful," she was saying.

"I will. I'm just going to get that pink suit I saw in your closet. I think you will look really nice in it."

"Leave it to you to pick out my favorite suit."

"I hope your mother and aunt like it." (I left, forgetting all about the man who had been following me.)

I got on the elevator, forgetting about my conversation with Susan. I was thinking about what shoes I should get to go with the suit. I remember how she liked everything to match. When I got down to the lobby, I didn't see the man coming in the revolving door.

I forgot all about Officer Jackson coming over to the hotel. My mind was on one thing —that was getting the suit for Susan's services. It was such a lovely day I decided to walk. It gave me some time to think about Susan and her services. This would be the last time I get to see her. My blue-eyed friend, I would miss her more than anyone I have ever known. The way we became instant friends in preschool. The way we could tell what each other was thinking and talking to each other and no one was the wiser. She was the sister I never had, and it was going to be hard saying goodbye tomorrow. Thinking of Susan, I didn't see the man following me. It wouldn't make a difference anyway because I didn't know him. I had never seemed him before.

I started to cry, thinking about my friend. I heard her ask me what was wrong. I started to answer, and she said, "No, just think about it, and I will hear you remember."

"I'm going to miss you. You were the only friend I ever had. I'm sorry I didn't recognize you that day coming out of the restaurant in Chicago." How did you get there anyway if you were already dead?"

"You brought me."

"I brought you?"

"Yes, you see, you were thinking about me at the moment of my death. So I came to you. I was thinking of you too. How I was missing you and wishing I could see you one more time because it had been a long time since I saw you last. I didn't know when I would get to see you again. And about how I hadn't stayed in touch with you and yet you were the only real friend I ever had. I loved you like you're my sister, but more than that. It was like you were a part of me, and I was missing the best part of myself. I'm so sorry.

"That alright, I should have come to New York to see you, but you knew how my parents were."

I was so deep in thought I hadn't realized I had gotten to Susan's apartment building. I went in and told the desk clerk that I was here to pick up an outfit for Susan.

"Yes, a course you can go right up. Do you need a key?"

"No, I have the key, thank you."

"Just let me say again how sorry we are about Ms. Brown; she was a charming young lady. She always had a friendly greeting for everyone."

"Thank you, Susan was always like that nice to everyone." I went to the elevator push the button to wait. It was right there. I got on and went up to Susan's apartment. I put the key in the lock, but the door was already open. There was a man there I hadn't seemed before. He was looking for something and didn't know I was in the room.

"Excuse me," I said. "May I help you with something? What are you looking for?"

He turned around; he had the bluest eyes I had ever seen. They were bluer than Susan's.

"Hello, you must be Susan's friend Veronica. How are you?" I'm sorry about Susan. "She was a charming girl."

"Yes, she was. Who are you?" Susan was talking in my head, "that's John she was saying, don't believe anything he says to you."

"Why not?" I thought.

"Trust me, Ronnie, just don't believe him."

"How did you know I was Susan's friend?" I asked him.

"She told me so much about you. You're even more beautiful than she said."

"And you are who?"

"I'm John, a friend of Susan. Surely she told you about me."

"What are you doing here?"

"I came to pick up some papers Susan was keeping for me. Perhaps you know where they might be?"

"Why do you think I would know where your papers are?"

"I thought with you and Susan being such good friends; she might have told you."

"No, she didn't. I just came to get something for the services tomorrow."

"Now, what might that be?" he asked.

"The pink suit in her closet," I said.

"Are you sure that all you came here for something for her services? It couldn't be a briefcase by any chance?"

"What briefcase? What are you talking about?"

"Be careful, Ronnie; he's not as nice as he's trying to pretend to be."

"I know he is frightening me."

"Susan didn't tell you anything about me and my business?"

"No, I haven't talked to Susan for some time. The last time I spoke to her, she didn't mention anyone in particular."

"Oh, and when was the last time you talked to her?"

"I don't know, maybe two or three years ago. Maybe even longer."

"That long? Are you sure?"

"Did you tell him about the things we used to do?"

"Yes. Oh, Ronnie, I didn't know it would come to this."

"What are we going to do, Susan?" I asked her.

"I don't know, but I'll try to come up with something."

"I told you that it had been a while since I talked to her," I said.

"Not even in that special way you two had of talking?"

"No, not even in that way."

"Now, if you will excuse me. I have some things to get for Susan's services tomorrow."

CHAPTER THIRTY-ONE

I turned to leave the bedroom, and he caught me by the arm. "You're not going anywhere until you tell me what Susan said about me."

"Nothing, I don't even know who you are."

"Will let me introduce myself; my name is John."

"John, what?"

"John will do for now."

"Hello, John, may I go and get Susan things now?"

"Just a moment, are you sure Susan didn't tell you anything about me or what kind of business I'm in?"

"No, if she had, I would remember."

I turned to go into the bedroom, and he grabbed my arm again. "You're not going anywhere."

"Let go of my arm. I told you I didn't know you, and by the way, you're acting; I would say Susan didn't know you either. She wouldn't be with someone as crude as you."

"Oh, no?"

"No, because Susan was a sweet and loving person. She would never associate with someone like you."

"What is that supposed to mean?" he asked.

"I mean, she was so sweet and caring and beautiful she wouldn't or couldn't be with someone like you."

He grabbed me and pushed me into a chair.

"What are you doing?" I told you I didn't know who you were. "I just came to get some clothes for Susan's service tomorrow."

"I knew what you said. I just don't believe you. Now tell me where the briefcase and I'll let you go."

"What briefcase? I don't know what you're talking about."

I think you do, so we'll just sit here until what she told you come back to you."

I didn't know what to do. I was looking around and saw Susan standing in the corner. Why is everyone asking me about a briefcase that I never heard of?

"Who been asking about the briefcase?" he wanted to know.

A man named Justin Wheeler. He came to my hotel and asked about it said you sent him.

"I told him what I just told you. I didn't know what he was talking about."

"Don't look up and don't say anything else, not yet. When you do speak, say just what I tell you," Susan was saying.

"Okay, but Susan, I'm afraid."

"I know I'm going to help you get out of this."

"How? he wants the briefcase, and it's not here."

"I knew. Have I ever let anyone hurt you before?"

"No, but you're dead now; how are you going to help me?"

"Just wait and see it'll be alright."

"John, the case is in the bedroom closet."

He looked around, "what did you say?"

"The briefcase is in the bedroom closet."

"No, it's not. I looked in there already, and it's not there."

"Yes, it is. It's in the back." I was saying in Susan's voice.

"In the back?"

"Yes, in the back." Susan was saying.

"You know you sound just like Susan."

"I do? I don't understand why you would say that. Susan and I sound nothing alike."

"You know you're not bad-looking, quite beautiful." He started toward me.

"Don't you want to go get the briefcase?" I asked again in Susan's voice.

"Yes, you stay right there and don't move." He went into the bedroom.

"Susan, I'm afraid, what should I do now?"

"Get up and go to the door as fast as you can." I got up and was almost at the door when John came out of the bedroom. He started to say something and looked up to see me across the room. Before I knew what had happened, he had grabbed my arm and turned me toward him.

"Where do you think you're going?" I told you to stay put.

"I told you where the briefcase was; why don't you let me go?" I asked in my voice.

"Because it was not there," he said.

"I'm through playing around with you. I want that briefcase, and I want it now."

"I don't know anything about a briefcase I told you. Please let me go." Before I knew what was happening, he had slapped me. I was stung. I had never been slapped before in my life, not by anyone. The kids didn't like me even when I was in school, but no one ever slapped me. My eyes swell up with tears. I was stung. I couldn't say a word; I just looked at him.

"Susan, I thought, Susan, did you see what he did to me? I've never been slapped in my life. What can I do but tell him where the case is?"

"No, don't worry, I'll take care of this." Susan was saying to me.

I listened, and the next thing I knew, Susan's voice was coming out of my mouth again.

"How dare you slap my friend, my sister? How dare you treat her like this? She said she didn't know where the briefcase was, so let her go now."

CHAPTER THIRTY-TWO

He was stung to hear Susan's voice coming out of my mouth, so angry.

"What kind of trick is this?" he asked.

"Susan, what are you doing? I didn't know you could do this," I was thinking.

"I never meant for any of this to happen. Ronnie, you must believe me."

"I do. Don't worry about it. Let's just get through this," I said.

I was looking at Susan's friend John. He was looking totally confused. I thought that if I could reach the door, I could get out of there. I heard Susan's voice in my head telling me now move while he's across the room. I started toward the door again, but before I could reach it, he was there, pulling me by my hair. I screamed.

"Where do you think you're going? I told you I want that briefcase."

"I don't know what you're talking about, I told you. Please let me go. I haven't seemed Susan in years; why do you think she would tell me about you or your briefcase?"

"I know she told you, and you're not leaving here until you tell me where it is."

"Susan, what are we going to do? Susan, are you here? Answer me, Susan. Please don't leave; I don't know what to do." But she had left. I don't know when she left; she just did. I started to cry.

"Susan, Susan, please come back. I don't know what to do." I began to talk out loud and didn't realize it. I thought you were my friend. I thought you would always be here for me, Susan; please come back.

"What are you doing?" John asked.

"What?"

"Why are you talking about Susan like that?"

"Like what?"

"Like she's here in the room."

"She, not. My friend has left me, and I will never see her again."

"I think you're crazy. Where is my briefcase? This is the last time I'm going to ask."

"I don't know. I keep telling you." I don't know why I kept up with the lie after Susan left me; it just seemed important that I did. I didn't see when he walked over toward me. I looked up to see a gun in my face.

I don't know what game you are playing, but I'm tired of fooling around. Tell me what I want to hear, or someone will plan your funeral tomorrow. He pulled back the hammer of the gun. I screamed before I realized I was going to do so.

There was a knock at the door. "Miss Smith, are you alright?"

"Who's that? he asked in a whisper.

I don't know. Only Susan's mother knew I was coming to get something for the services tomorrow.

"Miss Smith, can you hear me?"

"Tell him, yes. Say you are fine."

"Yes, I'm fine. I was just startled by something. It's okay now."

"Are you sure?" the voice on the other side of the door asked.

"Yes, I'm all right."

I didn't know that the police were having me followed. The person at the door was a police officer. He was following me because the police thought I knew more about Susan's death than I said. They didn't believe me when I said I hadn't seen her in years and that she came to me on the day she died. They thought I was a nut. They didn't believe the things I told them about Susan and me when we were children. I should have known they wouldn't believe me, but it never crossed my mind that they wouldn't. So they had me follow.

Mrs. Brown asked me to check on you. She said that you were coming to get clothes for your friend's services tomorrow, and you had been gone for a while, and she was worried that maybe it was a little much for you.

"No, I'm alright. I was just about to leave."

"Need any help?"

"No, I'll be right down."

"Okay, call if you should change your mind about the help."

"Alright, thank you."

"You know you're not getting out of here until you tell me what happened to that briefcase," John was saying.

"I told you I don't know what you're talking about."

That had been the officer at the door checking up on me. He had seemed me get on the elevator, but he had not seemed me come back down. I got up to get the suit for Susan's services. As I stood up to go to the bedroom, John hit me like no one had ever hit me before. In fact, I had never been hit by anyone before. I fell back down in the chair. It hurt so back I couldn't even cry; it surprised me that much. I sat there staring at him, unable to say a word. Until I finally realized what had happened.

"What did you do that for?" I asked him.

"I want to know where that briefcase is, and I want to know now."

"I told you I didn't know what you're talking about. I haven't seen Susan in years."

"You're lying. I know you saw Susan; how else would you know she had died?"

"Would you listen to yourself?"

"How could I see Susan if she was already dead? How can anyone see the dead?"

"You know what I'm talking about. I know you and Susan had this special thing between you; she told me about it."

"So what have that to do with me seeing or talking to her after she died?"

This seemed to make him angry he raised his arm to hit me again, but I saw it coming and moved out of the way this time. This only made him more furious. He hit me harder than the first time. This time, I cried out, and there was a knock at the door. "Miss Smith, are you okay? Is there someone in there with you?"

I opened my mouth to say yes, and John told me to say no. I looked at him, wondering what he would do next; would he hit me, would he shoot me. I didn't know. So I called out, "yes, there's someone here, and he has a gun."

"Why did you do that?" he asked.

"Because I don't want you to hurt me anymore. I have never been hit in life until you just did it twice."

The officer broke the door open and came in with his gun drawn. "Put your hands up," he told John.

"Are you alright? He asked, turning toward me. But before I could reply, John came forward and hit him in the head, knocking him out.

"I screamed, and John turned and said, this is not over and left the room."

CHAPTER THIRTY-THREE

I went to see if the officer was alright. I didn't know what to do, so I called Officer Jackson at the station, but he wasn't there. Then the door opened, and CJ was standing there. I ran to him, crying. "He's been hurt! And I didn't know what to do. He needs help."

Calm down, he said. "What happened?"

"I came to get something for Susan to wear, and he was waiting for me. Will not waiting for me, he didn't know I was coming, but he was here."

"Who is he?"

"He's the man Susan was seeing. He was looking for a briefcase that she was keeping for him."

"CJ was staring at me. You're hurt. What did he do?"

"I'm okay. The officer is more important than I am right now." He checked on the officer and called it in.

"He was looking for the briefcase you told me about where is it?"

"It's not here. It's back at the hotel." What happen to you?" I asked him.

"I was knocked down by someone who was running down the hall," he said.

"That was the man who was waiting in here for me."

"Do you know his name?"

"His name is John."

"What's his last name?" CJ wanted to know.

"I don't know, and he didn't say."

You were telling me about a briefcase earlier today. "Do you know what in it?"

"No, I don't," Susan told me to give it to you right away, but I forgot. I'll give it to you tomorrow.

"Why tomorrow?"

"There's something I need to do first."

"And what would that be?"

"Something Susan asked me to do. I can give it to you tonight if you can come by?"

"I will," he said. "But Veronica, no more fooling around. You will tell me everything you know about your friend's business."

"It wasn't a business; it was her job. I just found out about it yesterday."

"How? Who told you about this job?"

"I'll let you know later."

"Okay, would you like for me to take you to the hotel now?"

"Yes, please don't be angry with me. I'll tell you everything later. I promise, okay?"

CJ took me back to the hotel and left someone to keep an eye on me just in case John came back. Susan's mother and Aunt were out, so I went straight to my room, and there was Susan.

"I'm so sorry, Ronnie, by tomorrow, all this will be over. I know you are not used to things like this, but you are the only one who can help." Look at what he did to you? He's hurt you bad.

"That's okay; you were my best friend, and you still are. I love you, Susan, and if this will help to find who killed my blue eyes friend, I will do it no matter what it takes."

"Oh, Ronnie, I wish you could have come to New York with me after college. We could have had so much fun together. I love you, Ronnie, and I always will you. You will always be the sister I never had. Tell my mother I love her very much, and thanks for bringing you to New York with her."

"She won't believe you said that, but I will tell her," I said, smiling.

"Yes, she will. Now let's get finished with this mess."

"Have you made the copies yet?"

"No, not yet."

"Then, you should go do that now."

"But what if I'm followed?"

"You won't be, trust me," Susan said.

"I do," I replied.

"So go make the copies and bring them back here. I'll tell you what to do with them."

I went and did what Susan asked. When I got back, Mrs. Brown and her sister were there.

"Everything set for tomorrow?" I asked.

"Yes, all the family that could make it said they would be here."

"Good, are you going to be alright?" I asked her.

"Yes, I'm fine. What about you?"

"Yes, I'll just stay in the back tomorrow out of the way," I told her.

"You will do no such thing you were Susan's friend. You will set upfront with me."

"That's very nice of you, but what will your family think?"

I don't care what they think. You will sit with me, and that it."

"Thank you; I will be honored."

"I don't know why you even want that girl around," Melissa was saying. "You didn't even like her when she was a child."

I was wrong. She was the best thing that happened to my little girl. I just didn't know it then. I wish Susan had more friends or even a cousin like Veronica.

"You can't mean that!" Susan's aunt said in surprise.

"Yes, I do. I can see how much she truly loved Susan, and she still does. She was the only one who truly understood Susan, and Susan understood her. They were the best of friends; I just didn't understand why back then. But I know they had something special, and that was the love of a true friend. I'm sorry for the way I acted when they were children. They were always there for one another. I thought Veronica wanted something from Susan, but she didn't; she just loved her like a sister. I wish I had understood that then, but I didn't. I am so sorry for not understanding back then."

"That's okay, mom. Just listen to what Ronnie tells you now and believe her. I love you, mommy; thanks for being my mom."

"What was that? Gloria asked. I thought I heard Susan's voice saying that she loved me.

"You did, and she says thanks for bringing me with you," I told her.

Mrs. Brown smiled at me as a tear started running down her cheek.

I went back to my room. I didn't hear the conservation that went on in the other room.

"Susan? I got the copies. What do you want me to do with them?

"Give the copies to the police and mail the originals to yourself. Then, put them in a safe deposit box back in Chicago when you get back."

"Why?"

"For safe keeping just in case you need it."

"Why would I need it? What for?"

Just trust me, Ronnie. Have I ever done anything to hurt you before?

"No, I'm just frightened." (Thinking about what had happened today.)

"Don't be, and I'm here to protect you. No one is going to hurt you again. Call your friend to come and get the paper and briefcase now."

I got the number to Jean's restaurant and called her and asked her to call her brother for me.

"Why don't you call him yourself?" she wanted to know.

"He wasn't very pleased with me the last time I talked with him."

"Why? What happen?"
"Maybe I'll tell you later."
"Could you please call and ask him to come over?"
"Okay, I'll do it right now," she said
"Okay, I'll be waiting," I told her.

CHAPTER THIRTY-FOUR

I stay in my room. I didn't know how long it took for CJ to come. I just knew he wasn't happy to see me when he arrived. It hurt so much. I didn't mean to lie to him; Susan said it was better this way until everything was over. He treated me so cold, but I was used to being treated like this. So I put on a brave face to talk to him.

"Ms. Smith, I received word that you wanted to speak to me."

"Yes, I have something to give to you. Can you come into the other room, please? I'll keep the door open a bit. It imperative that you hear this and see what I have."

"Is everything all right, Veronica? Mrs. Brown asked as she and her sister came out of the other room.

"Yes, fine, Mrs. Brown, I mean, Gloria. I just need to talk to office Jackson for a second."

"Alright, we will get out of your way. Come on, Melissa, let's leave these two alone."

"Why? I thought this was your suite. "It's our suite," so let's go; she told her sister. They left so we didn't go to the bedroom.

"Could you please sit down?" I asked him.

"Why? To hear more lies from you?"

"No, I'm so sorry for not telling you the truth, but Susan said I had to wait, so I did."

"Susan? Susan Brown, your dead friend? When did she tell you this?"

"Two days ago, when I went to her apartment. She asked me to give it to you right away, but every time I was with you, I would forget."

"Why?" he asked

"That besides the point now, just let me get through with this," I told him.

So I told him everything from when I seemed Susan back in Chicago to when she appeared to me here. I told him she wanted me to know what happened to her and who did it. She told me what happened on her job. I told him the first person who got in touch with me was Felecia Jordan, who said she was a Susan friend. We went to lunch at your sister's place. You can check with her. I call to get the okay to go to Susan's apartment. And they said it was alright, so I went there, and when I got back here, there was a man down in the lobby wanting to talk to me who said his name was Justin Wheeler.

"Why didn't you call me or at least call the station?"

"Because Gloria and her sister came back while he was here, you can check with her if you want."

Susan came to me again and told me to give the briefcase to you again. But I forgot it again. Then I went to her apartment to get a suit for her services, and that was when a man named John was there. You should know you had me followed. The man who knocked you down was John. I came back here and did what Susan asked me to do.

"Can I ask you something?"

"What is it?"

Why do you keep calling your friend's funeral the service?"

"Because, if I call it anything but the service, I don't think I could handle it right now."

"So, where this briefcase you been telling me about?"

"Wait here. I'll go get it for you." I went into the bedroom, trying to keep myself together.

"Ronnie, what's wrong? Susan asked.

"I don't know. I didn't know I would feel like this."

"Like what?"

"Never mind, I'm about to give him the briefcase."

"Did you put the other papers away?"

"Yes, I mail them to myself," I told her.

"Are you okay?" Susan asked again.

"Yes." Let's just get this over with, so he can leave. I came back into the living room, here the papers and briefcase. I turn to leave.

"Wait, are you alright?" he asked.

"Fine, just tried. Will you be coming to the services tomorrow? It's at three o'clock."

"I don't know. I'll try," he said. Then he left without saying another word; Not even goodbye.

My head was hurting so badly from were the man John had hit me. Mrs. Brown came back. She looked at me, "Veronica? Are you alright?" she asked.

Yes, I just tried. I went into the bedroom and cried as I had never cried before. And I didn't understand why.

"Ronnie? Are you ok?" It was Susan.

"Oh, Susan, what have I done? The only man that ever made me felt special, and now he hates me."

"It will be alright, Ronnie."

"No, it won't. I have no one. You're gone, my parents are gone, there is no one back home who cares about me; what am I going to do?" Why did you have to leave me? Why couldn't you stay with me?"

"Because this is the way it had to be. I love you, Ronnie. I always will. I'll be there whenever you need me. Try not to be so sad. Everything is going to be alright."

I don't know how long I laid there crying and feeling sorry for myself; finally, I fell off to sleep. I dreamt about my parents in a way

I never saw them in life, especially my mother. She talked to me like she never did in life.

"Veronica? Don't cry. Everything is going to be okay." My mother told me.

"No, it not, you're gone, daddy's gone, and now Susan, there no one else to love me or want to be with me. I'm all alone." I told her as I dreamed.

"You're not alone; we have been here all the time; there was no way of letting you know until now. Oh, my wonderful, beautiful daughter, I'm so proud of you. Everything that you have accomplished listen to Susan, and do what she tells you and remember that your father and I are so proud of you."

I woke up not knowing where I was. Then I remember I was in New York for my best friend's funeral. I didn't know what time it was. I just got up and went to bed. I woke up in the middle of the night, and there was Susan just looking at me.

"Oh, Ronnie, I'm going to miss you so much. Remember the fun we used to have when we were young?"

"I remember no one wanted to sit by me or play with me or talk to me. They always called me your little *nigger* friend and said you were crazy to be around with me. They would say that you would catch something from me. But you were always there taking up for me and telling me not to worry about what they were saying that you would not let anyone hurt me. And you didn't. You were always there for me. You were my friend."

"You were my friend, Ronnie people just didn't understand us."

"I know. I'm going to miss you, Susan," I told her.

"And I you, Ronnie, I'll always love you."

"Good night Susan."

"Good night, Ronnie, Good-by," she whispers, and then she was gone.

CHAPTER THIRTY-FIVE

The next day was Susan's services. I didn't know what to expect, seeing I was the only black person expected to be in attendance.

The services were beautiful. There were more people than I thought would be there. All of Susan's family that I knew was there and some that I didn't. I tried to sit in the back, but Mrs. Brown wouldn't let me. So I sat up front with her. I looked for CJ, but he didn't come. I was sad about it, but I put on a brave face and got through the services. I couldn't believe the turnout, so many people were there. I kept looking for CJ, but he never came. Finally, the minister asked whether anyone had anything to say. Mrs. Brown asked me to say a few words.

"What do you want me to say?" I asked her.

"Say what in your heart, tell them what Susan meant to you."

I'll try. I went to the front, and I heard the people behind me starting to talk. I turned around to sit back down, but Susan looked at me, which was strange because she wasn't looking at anyone but me. "Go on, Ronnie, you can do it," she was saying. So I did.

"Good afternoon. My name is Veronica Smith. I was Susan's best friend. We grow up together. We meet in preschool. We were about four years old. I heard her say, "it's okay, Ronnie, it going to be alright." And we became friends that day. I love Susan. There's so much I could tell you about Susan, but a lot of you probably know her better than me, but I think I loved her more. I'll miss Susan. She will always be my Blue Eyes Friend. Thank you."

I sat down, everyone was looking at me strangely, but I didn't care that time. I looked for Susan; well done, she said, "I love you," and then she was gone.

"Thanks, dear, that was beautiful. I see more and more why you and Susan were such good friends. I wish I had understood early on, but I didn't."

"That okay. Those were times we lived in."

"You're so understanding. Will you stay in touch after this is over?" Gloria asked

"Yes, a course."

The services didn't last too much longer after that. I looked to see if CJ may have come after all, but he still wasn't there. I didn't go to the place where they laid her to rest. I wasn't coming back to New York (or so I thought). So I felt I didn't need to know.

Mrs. Brown stayed in New York for another day. Then she went back to Chicago. I stayed in New York for three days, and all that time, I didn't see CJ or Susan. It was as if I was alone in the city. I took care of packing up Susan's apartment for her mother. She had pictures of friends and family.

Then I found pictures of Susan and me when we were in preschool. It was one of the first pictures we took. We were standing there with our arms around each other. I remember the photographer telling us that we couldn't take our picture like that.

We each had to take one by ourselves. But Susan was having none of it. We want to take it just like this, she told him.

"Your parents will not be happy about this," he said. Then he called our teacher over, who tried to break us apart, but Susan still would not take the picture any other way. Well, go on and take it; we just have to deal with the parents when they see it.

"Okay," he said and took the picture with us standing with our arms around each other. I sat there staring at that picture. Remember how upset our mothers were. Susan's mother said I messed up her daughter's first school picture, and my mother said it was all Susan's fault. After that, they said we couldn't play with each other anymore. My mother even tried to get me moved into another class.

"I told you not to play with her when she was calling you Ronnie." But I like to be called Ronnie. That is not your name! "Your name is Veronica Marie Smith, not Ronnie. Do you understand me, Veronica?" Yes, mommy, I said.

That was that, as far as my mother was concerned. There were so many memories I just sat there going over them in my mind. Oh, how I was going to miss my blue eyes friend. I was deep in thought when the apartment door opened. It startles me.

"Veronica, I thought you had returned home. I know Susan's mother left a couple of days ago. I thought you went with her."

"Excuse me?"

"It's me. Felecia, Felecia Jordon."

I just stare at her.

"Felecia Jordon Susan's friend. We meet at lunch."

"Oh, yes, how you are?"

"Fine."

"What are you doing here?"

Like I said, "I thought you were gone, and I came to pack up Susan's things."

"Who told you I was gone? And who told you to pack up Susan's belongings? I know her mother didn't ask, so who told you to come here?"

"A friend."

"Who is this friend, and why did they think I was gone?"

"Just a friend, that's all."

"Maybe I should call your job and see if anyone knows that you are here."

"Well, if you don't want my help, then I'll leave."

"Help me? You didn't say you came to help me. You said that you came to do it."

"I'm leaving. You can do it by yourself. I was just trying to save you a little pain, that's all."

"I don't believe you."

"Believe what you want. I'm leaving." She slams the door behind her.

I didn't know what to do or who to call. Should I call the police or Gloria? I didn't know what to do. I wanted to call CJ, but I didn't. I didn't want to involve Gloria with this. I didn't know what was going on with Susan's friend John. So I stayed in at night and only went out in the daytime. I know that it didn't keep me safe, but I had to close Susan's apartment. The strange thing was I couldn't feel Susan present there anymore. It was as if this were a total stranger apartment. So I did what was asked of me, put what I could in storage, and gave the rest to charity.

No one bothers me, not the police, nor the man John who I was so afraid of, no one.

CHAPTER THIRTY-SIX

I was going to go to Jean's place for dinner. As I got to the restaurant, I looked in the window, and there was CJ with a woman. I didn't know what to do. Should I go in and pretend I didn't see him or go back to the hotel? I did want to see Jean before I left, but I turned around and went back to the hotel instead. When I got there, I looked in the mirror. I was crying. I didn't even know I was. I guess I was more hurt than I thought. I was trying to find something to watch on TV when there was a knock on the door.

I couldn't think who it might be. Everyone I knew was back in Chicago. I didn't know anyone in New York but CJ and Jean, but they were at the restaurant. I didn't want to answer it. I just wanted whoever it was to go away.

The knock came again, along with a voice. "Come on, Veronica, I know you're in there; open the door."

It was CJ.

I still just sat there, confused to hear CJ's voice coming from the other side of the door. Why was he here? What did he want?

"I'm not leaving until you open the door."

Could I be in some kind of trouble? I didn't think so. Then I heard Susan's voice very faintly telling me it was alright. I was even more confused because I thought she had left me after her services. The knock came again, a little harder this time.

"Veronica, open this door, or do you want me to break it down?"

I open the door, "what are you doing here? How did you know I was still here?"

Jean told me that you were coming to her place for dinner. So I went there to wait for you. But when you didn't show up, I figured you were hiding in your room. She said I needed to check and make sure you were alright.

"How did she know I was here?"

"I don't know. I thought you talked to her and made plans to be there."

"How did you know what room I was in? I changed rooms when Gloria left."

"I'm a cop, remember."

"You mean a police officer. I don't like the word cop; it doesn't stand for anything good."

"That still doesn't tell me how you knew what room I was in."

"I asked at the front desk."

"What can I do for you, Officer Jackson?"

"Oh, is that how it is now, Officer Jackson?"

"The last time I saw you, you were so mad at me you just walked away without a word, and the look on your face made me believe you didn't want to talk to me any longer. I was going to Jean for dinner then I saw you through the window with a young lady. I didn't know whether to go in or return to the hotel. So I did the latter, it was the best thing to do so I came back here.

"Why didn't you come in? Didn't you want to see me?"

"I didn't want to interfere."

"Why would you think you would be interfering?"

"You looked deep in conversation, and I didn't want to interrupt. So I say again, why are you really here? I told you all I could about Susan. She was my best friend. I'm so mad that I didn't keep in touch with her."

"First of all, you can stop with that Officer Jackson stuff."

"That who you are."

"Let's forget about that for now. Are you okay?"

"Yes, I was waiting for room service when you came."

"You can cancel it and go out to dinner with me."

"No, my dinner will be here any minute now."

While we were still talking, room service knocked on the door; I didn't say anything else. I just kept looking at him.

"If there were something wrong, you would tell me, wouldn't you?"

"Yes."

"Are you sure?"

"I said I would."

"Okay, then I will talk to you tomorrow."

I didn't say anything; I just looked at him.

"One more thing that young lady you saw me with was another police officer from my precinct. Officer Jones, first name Julie. So you see there nothing going on between us but work."

"Why are you telling this?"

"Thought you might want to know."

"Thanks, but your life is your life. It's not for me to get upset about who you see or don't see. I don't know why it should bother me in the first place."

"You are a strange one, Veronica Smith. Will you have dinner with me tomorrow night?"

"I don't know. I still have some packing to do at Susan's apartment; it might take longer than I think."

"When are you leaving?"

"In a couple of days, I guess."

"May I see you before you go?"

"I don't know. Can I think about it?"

He laughed and left, shaking his head.

I didn't know what to think. I would love to go to dinner with him. Should I go to dinner with him? I wanted to be with him right then. In fact, I never wanted him to leave me.

But I remember what my mother said, "if a man truly likes you, they would abide by your wishes and not push you into doing something you are not ready to do but would wait until you feel comfortable."

CHAPTER THIRTY-SEVEN

I don't remember eating. I couldn't remember what I ate.; I was too busy thinking about CJ. I sat on the couch, thinking about what had just happened. Wondering if CJ was as nice as I wanted to believe he was. There was a knock on the door. I got up to answer it, thinking that CJ had returned. Just as I reached to open it, I heard Susan cry, "don't open it."

"I did open it, and it was someone I didn't know.

"May I help you?"

"Veronica Smith?" I hear Susan tell me not to answer. "May I help you? I asked again?"

"I'm looking for someone named Veronica Smith. Are you her?"

Susan was saying; no, say no.

"Sorry, but I'm not."

"Do you know who she is?"

"I just got this room this morning. I lied."

"So, you don't know her?"

"No." I was surprised to see him believe me because he said thank you, the wrong room, and left. That's not what really surprised me, the surprise was I could hear Susan, not see her, but I could hear her.

Susan? Are you here?

I got no response. I thought that maybe I was imagined that I heard her; maybe it was only in my imagination. I gave no more thought about it. I started to get ready for bed; my mind had already backed on CJ.

I was on my way to the bedroom when Susan said: "be sure to lock the door." I thought I was just hearing things. Maybe it was just my imagination. I made sure the door was locked and thought no more about it when to bed.

I woke up to a cloudy day. I lay there looking out the window, wondering what the day would bring. I knew I only had about two hours of packaging to do at Susan's apartment, and the rest of the day, I would be free. I got up and went to take a shower, still wondering what the day would bring. I have never been to New York; I thought that maybe I would do some sightseeing go to all the places I heard about or saw on TV. As I was getting out of the shower, there was a knock on the door.

Room service.

Room service? I didn't order any room service. I wonder whether CJ did that last night before he left. Just a minute, I said as I started for the door. As I reached it, I heard Susan yell, don't open it, Ronnie.

I stop in my tracks. "Susan? Is that you?"

"Yes, it's me."

"I thought you had left me."

"I did for a little while, but I knew you would need me a little while longer."

"Why can't I open the door? Who out there?"

"Think, Ronnie, think about everything that then happens since you been here."

"Oh, my God. I turn to the door; I didn't order any room service."

"Complements of the hotel."

"I have been here a week. Why now?"

"Look, lady, if you don't want it, I can carry it back to the kitchen."

"No, I don't want it. It's too early for me to eat right now anyway, maybe later." I sat there, wondering what was going on.

Then I heard Susan talking to me, "I'm sorry, Ronnie, I thought that when you gave the briefcase to the police that this would be over, but I see it not."

"Where have you been, Susan? I called you, and you didn't answer me. What going on?"

"Ronnie, are you sure you gave the briefcase to the police?"

"Yes, I did just like you told me to do. What was in those papers that so important?"

"You didn't read the papers that were in the case?"

"You told me not to. You said that it would be better if I didn't know what was in them. So I just made the copies liked, you said."

"Ronnie, I'm so sorry I got you into all this mess, but you were the only one who could help. I need you to talk to your friend CJ. I need to know you are safe."

"Susan, I need to know what is in those papers that you asked me to keep for you."

"I guess it's time that I tell you. Ronnie, I do know a little more about John's business than I let on."

"Why didn't you tell me? Why are you telling me now?"

"I didn't mean for any of this to happen. I didn't know he would kill me."

"Didn't know who would kill you?"

"John, John killed me because of the papers in that briefcase. So now you have them, at least he thinks you have them, and he will do anything to get them back."

"What can I do, Susan? I don't even know what in those papers."

"I know Ronnie. I'm so sorry I should have realized when I asked you not to look that you wouldn't. I forget how trusting you are."

"What am I going to do, Susan? He doesn't believe that I don't have that briefcase."

"Don't worry, Ronnie. I won't let anything happen to you."

"But what going to happen to me? I don't know what's going on. Why did you get me involved in all this-this-this stuff?"

"I don't know, I was thinking of you all that day and decided to call you later that day because I needed a friend to talk to at the time, and you were my best friend. I was dialing your number when I was killed."

"That okay, Susan. It's going to be alright."

"See, you are the one who needs protecting, and you are still worried about me. There no more they can do to hurt me; it's you who we need too protected."

"What can I do?"

"Can you stay in today and not go anywhere?"

"That's not possible. I have to finish packing up your apartment and do the final things your mother asked me to do. I plan on going home tomorrow."

"Ronnie, I don't want anything to happen to you."

"I'll be careful."

"Can you put going home off for a couple of days?"

"I wish I could, but I got to get back to work on Monday. I didn't know I would be gone this long."

"Okay, but be careful, Ronnie."

"I will. Maybe I'll call CJ just in case. Will that make you feel better?"

"Yes, but please be very careful; you see what these people can do."

I finish getting dressed and want out. It was about twelve forty-five. I hadn't realized Susan and I had been talking for so long. I thought about going to Jean's for lunch then finished things at Susan's apartment. When I got there, I couldn't believe what I was seeing. Someone had destroyed everything from the kitchen to the bedroom, even the bathroom. I stood there, not believing what I was seeing.

"Susan? Susan! Can you hear me?"

"Yes, I can."

I turned around, and there was Susan. Not only could I hear her, but I could also see her standing there. She was wearing the outfit

I picked out for her services. I was surprised to see her there. I just stared at her.

"What's wrong, Ronnie? Why are you looking at me like that?"

"I can see you, and you still look beautiful."

"Why did you call me?"

"Look at this apartment. Who could have done this?"

"Think Ronnie, what did I tell you a little while ago? These people are dangerous? You need to get out of here right now."

But it was too late. I turn to go, and someone hit me in the head, and I blackout. When I woke up, I didn't know where I was. I looked around and couldn't see anyone. Susan, I thought, are you here? Yes. What happens? Where am I? Who are these people? What do they want with me? The briefcase. But I don't have it. I gave it to the police like you asked me to. I know, don't worry, I'll think of something. They're coming back. Pretend like you're still out.

The door opened, and I closed my eyes. And sit listening to what they were saying. Good, she's still out. They blindfold me. Stupid, I thought they should have done that before they brought me here.

Whatever you hear, Ronnie, it's not me. Susan, are you still here? I'm not going to leave you; just remember, not me.

CHAPTER THIRTY-EIGHT

Okay, let's get on with this; just make it believable.
"Veronica?" No, Ronnie, someone whispered.
Ronnie? Ronnie Yes, oh, I'm sorry (not me, Susan was saying).

"Susan, it that you?"

"Yes."

"Why did you call me, Veronica? You never call me Veronica."

"Why are you here? We had your services two days ago."

"Ronnie, I need to know what you did with the briefcase."

"What briefcase?"

"The one I gave you to keep for me."

"You didn't give me any briefcase to keep for you."

"Susan, I haven't seemed you in years, don't you remember? (Not me, Susan was saying in my mind).

Susan, I'm so surprised that you would get mixed up with something like this, whatever this is, and to get me involved. It's not like you."

"Susan? No answer."(I was talking to the person pretending that they were her.)

"They're leaving now, Susan was saying. Don't say anything yet. I don't need my mouth to talk to you.

"How could you get me mixed up in this? I never did anything remotely like this; what going to happen?"

"I don't know. But we got to get you out of here. Did you tell anyone what you are doing today?"

"Yes. I told CJ I was going to finish packing up your apartment."

"Were you to meet him later?"

"No, I told him I would call him. How will I get out of here? I don't know anything."

"I'm so sorry, Ronnie, for getting you into this."

"Stop saying that. I know it not your fault."

They're coming back.

"Ronnie, I'm back. Are you okay?"

"Can we stop pretending that you're Susan because you're not?"

She knows. You might as well take the off mask. It was John, Justin Wheeler, and Felecia Jordan. Ms. Smith, we knew Susan gave you a briefcase. We want to know where it is?

I told you I didn't know anything about a briefcase. I haven't seen Susan in years, why don't you believe me.

Because she told me about the things you did when you were children, and I thought it was interesting.

That's just it. We were children.

Then how did you know she was dead?

Her mother told me. That's why I'm here. Her mother asked me to come with her because we were friends when we were kids.

"And you came?" he asked.

"Yes."

"Why?" he asked.

"Why? Because Susan was my best friend. I love her like a sister."

"Like a sister, and yet you want me to believe you hadn't talked to her in years."

"I don't care what you believe. Susan live here in New York. I lived in Chicago; you tell me how many times she came home?"

John stood staring at me, trying to figure out if I was telling the truth.

"How much time did you two spend together? She loved you and wanted to spend all her time with you."

"How do you know if you didn't talk to her like you said? How do you know?"

"Because I knew Susan, I can look at you and see how much she must have loved you. I can look at you and see you loved her too. He stood there for a minute, turned, and walked out the door.

CHAPTER THIRTY-NINE

Veronica was trying to figure a way to get loose and get out without getting hurt. She was trying to work the ropes loose. That was very smart of you, Ronnie. How did you think of that so fast?

"Because of it's true, you did love him, and he loved you too. I know you, Susan; he had to be someone very special for you not to come home, not even to see your mother."

"You're right, Ronnie. You never cease to amaze me. You always could pick up on people better than I could."

"Will I still need to get out of here?"

"I wish I could help you in some way."

"Susan, I love you, but can you let me think for a minute?"

I heard her laugh. Think I kept saying to myself. Then I remember Jean.

Jean!

"Jean? Who's Jean?" Susan asked.

"She CJ sister she doesn't know it, but we made a connection on the first day we meet. I don't know if I can do it again. I'm so far from where she is. It's not like you and me when we were kids; it came so naturally for us; it was like it was meant to be for us."

"Give it a try, Ronnie. It can't hurt," Susan said.

I tried calling Jean, but it didn't work. It's not working.

"Try again, Ronnie. Shut your eyes and concentrate."

I closed my eyes and pictured Jean. There she was in the kitchen of her restaurant. I smiled. This is going to freak her out, I thought.

"Jean? Jean?" I could see her turning around to one of her cooks.

"Did you say something?" She asked.

"No, I didn't say anything," he said.

I called her again, "Jean, I need your help."

"Are you sure you didn't say anything?"

"No, you must be hearing things," he said.

"Jean, it's me, Ronnie. I need your help; call CJ and tell him I've been kidnapped."

"I'm not calling CJ; he's going to think I'm crazy."

"Please, Jean, I need your help."

"What?" she said out loud.

"No, don't talk, just listen. I'm in trouble, some men have taken me, and I don't know where."

"What are you talking about?" she said out loud.

The cook turned. "I didn't say anything."

"Sorry, I was thinking about something."

"Don't talk with your mouth. Just think of what you want to say. I'll hear you."

"How is this happening?"

"I'll explain later. Right now, I need you to call your brother so he can help me."

"Where are you?"

"I don't know. They knocked me out and brought me to this place."

"Okay," she said and turned to leave. Telling the cook she had to go and would back as soon as possible that something just can up.

"Hurry Jean, they're gone now, but they will be back soon, and I don't know what they're going to do. I'm so afraid; they're looking for something I don't have."

"I must be losing my mind."

"No, yours not."

"Okay, I will call him right now. How will you know what he said?"

"Just concentrate on me, and then you can tell me what he said."

"Okay, hung in there."

Just then, they can back in. What were you doing? Talking to Susan?

"No, how can I talk to her when she's dead?"

"So, what are you doing?"

"Praying that you don't hurt me again."

"You're a gorgeous woman. Why would you think I would hurt you? John asked.

"Because you did once, and you want something I can't give you."

"I am beginning to believe you, Veronica Smith. The thing is, what can I do with you now? You may not have what I want, but you know too much now."

"Know to mush about what? I don't even know what you are talking about."

"That too bad, you are beautiful, and that's the problem."

"You could let me go and finish package up Susan's apartment."

"No, I can't do that, Ms. Smith. You know too much," he said.

"About what? I don't know anything!" I yell at him.

"Relax, you're going to be here for a while. Would you like something to eat?"

"No, thanks."

"Hurry Jean, I'm so afraid!"

It seemed like it took Jean forever to get back to me.

"Ronnie, I did what you asked, but he said he needs more. I don't think he believes me. What can I tell him to make him believe me?"

"Let me think. Tell him this, I thought about it, and yes, he can see me before I leave tomorrow. Tell him I think about him more than anyone I know that if he can find me, I want to see him very much."

"Are you crying?" Jean asked.

"No, it's just I need him, and I never thought that I would need anyone or love anyone," I said in a whisper.

"Tell him I need him to find me, and he can't let anyone know he's looking for me, or they will kill me. They're trying to decide what to do with me. Tell him it's about the briefcase I gave him." Please hurry, Jean.

"I will, Ronnie. Please hang in there." She was crying

"Don't cry, Jean; it's alright."

They came back. "Get up, Ms. Smith; we're going for a little ride."

"Can't you be a bit more original? Try a new line; it may sound better than going for a ride."

"Hurry Jean, they're taking me somewhere else." The more frightened I became, the easier it became to talk to Jean.

CHAPTER FORTY

Jean went to talk to her brother again. "CJ, you got to help Ronnie right now. She's in trouble."

"Where is she?"

"That's just it. I don't know."

"How do you know she's in trouble? Did she tell you?"

"Yes, in a way."

"What do you mean in a way?"

"Some guys took her from her friend's apartment about two hours ago, and now they won't let her go."

"Took her? Took her where?"

"I don't know. She doesn't know either."

"Then how do you know someone took her?"

"You're not going to believe this, but she told me."

"Told you how?" CJ wanted to know.

"Here goes. I was in the kitchen of the restaurant when she called me."

"Called you? On the phone? What the number we can have it trace."

"Not on the phone exactly," Jean said.

"If not on the phone, how do you know she been taking?"

"That's what I'm trying to tell you. That thing you told me about her friend Susan and her? Will, apparently, we can do it too, Ronnie and me."

"How is that possible?" he asked in wonder.

"I don't know. She told me to tell you, yes; she would love to see you before she leaves tomorrow."

"Was she leaving?"

"Yes."

She said to tell you she thinks about you more than anyone she knows, and CJ she was crying she afraid that they were going to kill her. And you know what funny?" I started to cry, and she told me everything would be alright and not to cry.

"She said you need to hurry because they're moving her someplace else."

"Oh yeah,' she said; you can't tell anyone, or they will kill her for sure. Do you believe me, Cleophus? Jean wanted to know.

"Now, I do. You only call me by my name when you're very upset."

"Thank you for believing me. So what are you going to do?"

"You go back to the restaurant. I'll take care of this."

"Are you going to find her?"

"I'm going to do my best."

"No, your best isn't good enough. This time, you got to do better than your best."

"Believe me, Jean; I will. You go back to work, and I'll keep you posted on what happens, okay."

"I guess it has to be. Please find her."

"I will."

"Ronnie, I told him. He said he would find you."

"Thanks, Jean, but I don't know if he can. They're taking me someplace else, and I don't know where. I don't know this city, so it could be anywhere."

"So, what can I do?"

"Nothing, but thanks for trying. Tell your brother that I love him. It was so nice meeting you."

"Ronnie, you can't give up. You just can't. Ronnie? Ronnie?"

I wouldn't answer her; there was no more she could do.

"Susan, are you there?"

"Yes. Ronnie, I'm not going to leave you. I love you. You were my best friend, the only person who understood me."

"Susan, I'm afraid. What is it like to be dead?"

"Don't talk like that. You're not going to die."

"Well, I don't know. They're taking me someplace, and I don't know where. There no way I can let anyone know where I'm at."

Jean call her brother on her cell phone. "CJ, you got to hurry, they're moving her someplace else, and she doesn't know where. Please, please find her. After she told me they were moving her, she started talking about it was nice meeting us and that she loved you."

"Don't worry, Jean, we will find her."

"We?" She said not to tell anyone that they would kill her for sure. "Why did you tell? She trusted you. She trusted you to find her. Why did you tell?"

"Jean, calm down. No one knows I told anyone else I'm a police officer; remember, don't worry, everything will be alright. Now stop crying and go to work."

"I'm not crying."

"Yes, you are. I haven't heard you cry like this since Mom and Dad die."

Jean looked in the mirror to see she was crying. "I'm sorry." It's just I don't know—-

"Don't worry about it. I love her too. I'll find her."

CHAPTER FORTY-ONE

CJ didn't know when he fell in love with Ronnie, but he had, and no one was going to take her from him, not now. He wants to explore this thing he felt for Ronnie because he had never felt this way before. He went back into his captain's office. "We got to find Veronica Smith, captain. I got information that they are going to move her to another place."

"Where are you getting your information from, Jackson?" Are you in touch with her?

"My sister. She said she been in contact with Ms. Smith."

'Where did she tell you she was?"

"That's the problem she doesn't know. Ronnie has never been in the city before."

"Ronnie, is it now?"

"Ms. Smith, that was what I meant to say. Ms. Smith."

"Why would anyone want to take her?"

"It's about the briefcase we discuss."

"I thought you gave that case to the feds?"

"I did, but the people who have Ms. Smith don't know that. They don't even know if she ever had it. They're trying to get her to admit she knows where it is. They believe that she knows but is not telling. But she doesn't."

Call for you, Jackson. Says she your sister.

"Jean? What the matter?"

"Cleophus, have you found Ronnie yet?"

"No, I was talking to the captain."

"The captain?" She said not to tell anyone.

"I had to; I need all the help I can get to find her."

"Please hurry; she sounded so frightened when she talked to me."

Spoke to you? Has she talked with you again?

"Yes, somehow, we can talk to one another.

How are you able to speak to her?"

"I don't know. I just know she told me to think, and she can hear me."

"I think it's the man John, her friend Susan was seeing, and his friend Justin who has her."

"How do you know that?"

"I don't know; I just think it him and some of his friends."

I didn't know what was going on. Why was this happen to me? Susan, are you there?

There was no answer. So I'm in this all alone. I thought about contacting Jean again but decided not to. I didn't want to get her any more involved than I already had. I sat there, wondering what was going on—thinking about all the things that had happened to me. Wanting CJ to come and rescue me, but that wasn't happening.

I heard them coming back; we could take her back to the apartment; no one would look for her there. How are we going to get her in without being seen? We can take her up the back way. No one will even know she's there.

I was still blindfolded, and someone took me by the arm lift me out of the chair. We went down some stairs that I hadn't noticed before. I was trying to remember every sound and step we took just in case I could inform Jean where I was so she could get help. We got in a car funny. I didn't remember getting in a car to come here.

"That because you were on conscience," I heard Susan say.

"Susan, are you back?" "Yes."

"Where did you go?'

"I went to see your friend Jean. To let her know what was happening.

"How?"

"You were right, Ronnie; she can hear not only you but me too. I told her to tell her brother to hurry because they were moving you. I think she thought it was you talking to her."

"Where are they taking me? Do you know?"

"Back to my apartment; they think they'll be safe there. They don't realize that the police is looking for you."

"I told Jean to tell CJ not to tell anyone. What if they find out the police are looking for me? They're going to kill me. I don't want to die."

"You're not going to die, trust me, Ronnie. I got you in this mess, and I will get you out some how. I will get you out."

They parked the car in the garage and went up the back so no one would know I was there.

"Jean, tell CJ to hurry. I think they brought back to Susan's apartment."

We enter the apartment. And I heard what I believed to be another man.

"What going on? Why did you bring her back here?"

"Did you find the briefcase?"

"No, I looked all over this place; there nothing here. What are we going to do with her?" he asked.

"I don't know yet. I'll come up with something."

I was so afraid I started to tell them that I had given the briefcase to the police.

"No," Susan said. "They're almost here hung in there, Ronnie. You're doing great. I knew I could count on you. Just a few more minutes."

I thought about Jean. Hurry Jean they brought me back to Susan's apartment, and they are trying to decide what to do with me. Please tell CJ to hurry. They brought me in a back way, so no one knows I'm here.

"I told him, Ronnie, they're on their way."

"Tell them to be quiet, so they won't know they're coming." So, I sat there praying that CJ would get there in time. And that he would not get hurt. I wanted to tell him I loved him and that I loved him from the moment I saw him. But I was just afraid to let him know. I didn't know how to act or what to say, so I said nothing.

Lord, please let me be able to tell him how much I do love him. I was so deep in thought I hadn't realized that the police had arrived and was coming through the door. I sit there, blindfolded, praying, and thinking about CJ.

I thought I heard someone asking was I alright. But I couldn't be sure I was so deep in thought. I felt hands lifting me. Jean, I shouted, please help me; they are about to do something to me.

"Ronnie, are you alright? Ronnie, can you hear me? Are you alright?" He was taking the blindfold off, and I was looking into the face of Officer Jackson.

He looked at me and smiled, "are you okay?"

"Oh yes," I said with tears running down my face. "Oh, yes."

He untied me and put his arms around me, and gave me the biggest hug I had ever received in my life. He whispers, "I'm never letting you go" in my ear. I was so lost in his arms that I hadn't noticed that there were other officers in the room, and they had Felecia Jordon, Justin Wheeler, John Albertson, and the man who had been following me since I got to New York.

"Thank you for finding me."

"That alright; it's my job."

"Is that all it meant to you a job?"

"No. I think I'm falling in love with you, Veronica Marie Smith."

"And I think I'm falling in love with you, Office Cleophus Jackson." He smiles

www.ingramcontent.com/pod-product-compliance
Lightning Source LLC
La Vergne TN
LVHW011712060526
838200LV00051B/2874